ONE OF FOUR

WORLD WAR ONE THROUGH THE EYES OF AN UNKNOWN SOLDIER

TWENTIETH CENTURY WAR STORIES

TRAVIS DAVIS

My Random Thoughts

One of Four – World War One Through the Eyes of an Unknown Soldier

Copyright © 2024 Travis Davis

(My Random Thoughts, LLC)

First Edition: 2024 (Revised 2025)

Printed in the United States

ISBN – 13: 979-8-9901382-0-9 (Paperback)

ISBN – 13: 979-8-9901382-1-6 (Hardcover)

ISBN – 13: 979-8-9901382-2-3 (ebook)

Published by My Random Thoughts, LLC

Bulk orders of this book may be obtained by contacting My Random Thoughts, LLC at www.randomthoughts.llc

Public Relations Dept. – My Random Thoughts, LLC

972-897-8872

travis@randomthoughts.llc

My Random Thoughts, LLC

972-897-8872

travis@randomthoughts.llc

AUTHORS NOTE

Some of the incidents and characters in this book are based on historical events and real people.

TWENTIETH CENTURY WAR STORIES

TRAVIS DAVIS

ACKNOWLEDGMENTS AND DEDICATIONS

This book was a labor of love to write and research. I want to thank Paul Behringer for his assistance in *One of Four*. Paul is a senior fellow at the Center for Presidential History at Southern Methodist University. He is also a historian with the Henry Jackson Foundation, supporting the Defense POW/MIA Accounting Agency.

In addition to Paul, I want to thank my wife, Martina, our daughters, Kandyce and Brittany, our son, Tyler, and son-in-law, Jon, for sticking with me in this adventure and constantly hearing, "Did you know that in World War I…"

I also want to acknowledge all the Tomb of the Unknown Soldiers Sentinels of the 3rd Infantry Old Guard, past and present, who have stood guard over one of the most treasured and hallowed grounds in the United States, twenty-four hours a day, three hundred and sixty-five days a year, since July 2nd, 1937.

PREFACE

HÔTEL DE VILLE (CITY HALL): CHALONS-SUR-MARNE, FRANCE

In October 1921, the remains of four unknown soldiers were exhumed from grave sites at four American cemeteries in France, Aisne-Marne, Meuse-Argonne, Somme, and St. Mihiel by teams from the Quartermaster Corps assigned to each location. After the remains were unearthed, each one underwent a thorough, detailed forensic examination to ensure they died of wounds sustained in combat and their identities could not be determined. The location of their deaths, original burial locations, and uniforms were used to ensure they were U.S. troops.

After the examination, the mortuary teams prepared the bodies. They were placed in flag-draped identical caskets and shipping cases. The reason for identical caskets and shipping cases was to ensure an impartial, truly random selection of the unknown soldier. The U.S. government did not initiate this practice. Great Britain and France buried one soldier each on November 11th, 1920. They used the same selection criteria for their unknowns.

On October 23rd, 1921, all four flag-draped caskets containing the bodies of the unknown soldiers arrived by truck at Hôtel de Ville (City Hall) of Chalons-sur-Marne, a small city with a population of 32,000. The four unknowns lay in identical caskets on top of their new shipping cases. One of the four would be selected to be interred at the Tomb of the Unknown Soldier at Arlington National Cemetery in Virginia. Inside the city hall, the four unknowns lay in their identical caskets.

An Army sergeant was chosen to select the casket. Sergeant Edward F. Younger of Headquarters Company, 2nd Battalion, 50th Infantry, American Forces in Germany. He was given the honor of choosing the unknown the following day based on his actions in the war. He was a hero, having received the Distinguished Service Cross, the second-highest award that can be given to a service member. He was also wounded in the war and was known for his bravery after being discharged from the Army on October 29th, 1919. The next day, he reenlisted and was assigned to the 50th Infantry in post-war Germany.

On October 24th, 1921, he was given a spray of white roses by a French father who had lost two sons in the war. While Sergeant Younger walked around the caskets, a band played a hymn in the background. He did this four times until he stopped and placed the spray of roses on a single casket, indicating his selection. As he stood in front of the casket, a feeling of sorrow mixed with pride, and then a sense of calm came over him, a feeling he had not felt in years.

He stepped back from the casket, saluted the unknown soldier, and stepped aside. U.S. and French officials walked forward and paid their respects. The spray of roses would remain with the unknown soldier and be interred with him.

Once the ceremony was completed, the casket of the unknown soldier was placed on a horse-drawn caisson and taken through the streets of Chalons-sur-Marne to the local railway station. Along the route, citizens lined the streets to bid farewell to the unknown soldier. But the local population knew him. He was one of the heroes who gave his life fighting for their country. Many wept as the horse-drawn caisson passed.

The casket of the unknown was placed in a special funeral train approved by the French government at the railway station. Once loaded, the train traveled through Paris to the port city of Le Havre. While the train traveled, crowds stood again to pay their respects. Some waved, others saluted, but all prayed for his soul.

At Le Havre, the casket of the unknown was carried aboard the *USS Olympia* for the trip across the Atlantic Ocean. On November 9th, 1921, the ship arrived at Washington Naval Yard. All the service chiefs, the Secretary of War, and the General of the Armies, John J. "Blackjack" Pershing, stood to watch as the casket of the unknown was removed from the ship.

The casket was placed on a horse-drawn caisson led by the *3rd Cavalry Regiment* for its journey to the Capitol Rotunda until November 11th, 1921. President Harding and over 90,000 ordinary citizens paid their respects as he lay in state.

On a cold morning, November 11th, 1921, exactly three years after the war ended, the casket carrying the unknown soldier made its final journey home and its final resting place from the Capitol Rotunda through Washington, D.C., across the Potomac River to Arlington National Cemetery. Escorting the unknown were the president, General Pershing, and eight highly decorated veterans. The eight consisted of five Army soldiers: an artilleryman, a cavalryman, a combat engineer, an infantryman, Sergeant Samuel Woodfill, a Medal of Honor recipient, and a member of the Coastal Artillery Corps. The two remaining veterans were from the Navy, and one was a Marine, Sergeant Ernest A. Janson, a recipient of the Medal of Honor.

That day, the unknown soldier was laid to rest under a simple marble slab, which is now known as the Tomb of the Unknown Soldier.

World War I Western Front Summer/Fall 1918

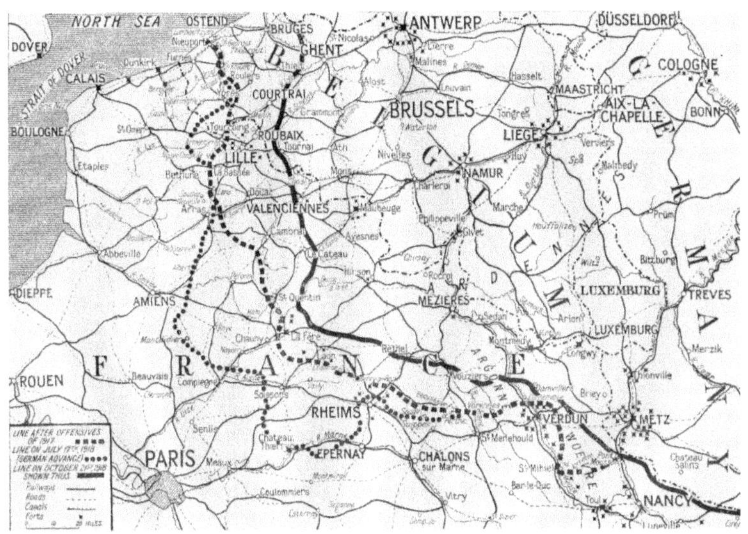

CHAPTER 1

A SOLDIER'S DIARY

NOMENY, FRANCE - OCTOBER 1918

Camille Durand woke to the distant sound of artillery—too far for her to be concerned. It wasn't the first time she had woken to that noise; it had become all too familiar since the war began four years ago. The day was cloudy and late fall in 1918, with a nip in the air and winter approaching quickly. Her father was off fighting the Germans, having joined the French army in early 1915, and he hadn't been home in months. After the massacre of sixty-three residents on August 20, 1914, in a small village in northern France, he couldn't stand by and watch his country be destroyed. Neither she nor her mother knew his exact whereabouts; all they knew was that he was on the front and alive, as indicated in his last letter, which had been two weeks prior. Her mother had become somewhat of a recluse since her father left for war. The stress of the conflict had taken a toll on her. Camille had been just a child when he went to fight the Germans. Since then, she had blossomed into a teenager full of energy, compassion, curiosity, independence, and a love for her country—a daughter any father could wish for. She missed her father deeply. He used to take her on long walks through the forests and fields, teaching her about nature, animals, and how to pick mushrooms. Her eyes would tear up whenever she thought of him, wishing he were home.

Her house had been in her father's family for over a hundred years. It was situated along the Aire River in a small village. The once-beautiful town had been ravaged by years of war, and now the nearly abandoned village lay in ruins, with skeletal buildings that seemed likely to collapse if subjected to a strong wind. What were once beautifully ornate structures, some dating back to the Renaissance and Neoclassical periods, that were filled with shoppers, families, and goods, were now empty and decaying—bricks and fragments of those charming buildings scattered across virtually indistinguishable streets. Walking down the street required considerable balance and coordination. In addition to the bricks strewn along the path, there were shell craters and pieces of lumber everywhere to navigate around or over. Her home didn't escape the war. It had been struck multiple times by machine gun fire and shrapnel from artillery shelling. Yet, it stood as a testament to the quality of its construction. Most other houses were abandoned, and the families that once lived in them were long gone. However, her mother vowed to remain until her husband returned. She would not be forced from her home.

Camille got off the bed and headed downstairs, hungry and dreaming of a large breakfast with fruit, cheese, meats, and fresh bread. However, there wasn't much her mom could buy or trade at the local markets. Most of the chickens, pigs, goats, and other farm animals had been slaughtered. The army took all the horses to transport equipment and weapons. Fresh vegetables and fruit were nearly impossible to find, yet she and her mother managed to survive. Whenever she could gather enough flour, she would make bread. Camille loved to bake; it was a form of relaxation that allowed her mind to wander about what could be.

She sat at the kitchen table, eating a slice of stale bread—it was all she had. Afterward, Camille returned to her room to prepare for another day of survival.

She sat on her bed, continuing to dream about life before the war, where she would go outside and play with her friends. All of them either moved away or were killed in the war. She wondered if she would ever see any of them again. Her days were filled with reading, helping around the house, and finding food. Her mother assured her that they would maintain a clean home no matter what the war brought. She would always say, "Cleanliness is next to godliness." A devoted Catholic, her mother often took out the family Bible and read verses from it

Camille also dreamed of what could be after the war and wanted to go to Paris. But today felt different. She couldn't explain it and didn't know whether it was a good or bad feeling. Maybe it was from the lack of machine guns firing in the distance last night or deep, uninterrupted, peaceful sleep. Yet she knew in her heart the day would be like every day since the war started. Why would it be any different? She decided to lie back in her warm bed. After a few minutes, she finally got out of her cozy bed, finished getting dressed, and walked to the glassless window. She pulled the torn curtains to the side.

In the distance, a small group of American soldiers advanced across a barren, artillery-cratered wasteland that had once been a lush, grassy field filled with beautiful, bright yellow daffodils, occasional oak trees, and a small herd of cattle. She waved at them, but they didn't wave back. She could tell they were American soldiers by their uniforms. She loved them. They had traveled thousands of miles and left their families to fight for their country, France.

A country they might not have heard of, or maybe they read about France in a book, or perhaps a place they would have loved to visit at another time. Sometimes, when an American patrol came close enough to her house, she would step outside to greet them. However, if the Germans caught her interacting with them, they would kill her and her mother. Even at a young age, Camille was rebellious. In return, they would give her some of their rations, such as bread, meat, or sugar, if they had any. To her, it seemed like they always had enough food. They always smiled, but there was something behind those smiles. Maybe they were just homesick, missing family or friends. At such a young age, what she saw behind their faces was exhaustion, pain, fear, and suffering that no one should have to endure. But still, their smiles brightened her mood, and she thought maybe, just maybe, her smile lifted their spirits.

Camille continued to watch the patrol advance when she heard the sounds of machine gun fire and artillery. They were closer than the ones she had heard in previous days. She crouched behind her bedroom wall, peeked over the window ledge, and observed the soldiers moving across the cratered field. They were running now, trying to avoid the machine gun fire while searching for any cover from the incoming bullets and shells. One soldier sprinted toward a comrade who was already wounded. As the shells began to fall, the soldier jumped on top of the fallen soldier, shielding him from the incoming rounds. As she watched, the same soldier knelt and fired toward the machine gun nest. She turned her head, unable to watch any longer. The brave soldier was getting hit by machine gun fire and shrapnel from the shelling.

They had walked into an ambush.

She ducked behind the wall as rounds found their targets and the shells began to explode. Boom, boom, boom—the vibrations shook the wall, accompanied by the blasts from the shells crashing into the ground. Her eardrums throbbed, and she covered her ears with her hands. She screamed, "Stop, stop!"

She buried her head in her hands. Her whole body trembled as she crouched behind the bedroom wall. Pieces of the ceiling fell to the floor. The vibrations were so intense that she wondered if the house would implode and crush her, yet she didn't move. The air was filled with dust and a musty smell. When the machine gun fire ceased and the barrage decreased, she raised her head to look over the window ledge. As the smoke and dust settled, all she could see were the craters left by the shelling. In the blink of an eye, the patrol she had been watching took almost a direct hit from the German artillery. As the air cleared further, none of the soldiers was visible. It was as if they vanished, vaporized.

She looked in the direction from which the soldiers had come, but there were no follow-on soldiers—nothing and no one. The artillery shifted to the right and continued for a few more minutes. The machine gun fell silent.

She sat with her back against the wall, crying. Once the artillery subsided, after what felt like a lifetime, she no longer heard any more machine gun fire. She got up, ran down the stairs, passed her mom in the living room, and left the house.

"Camille, où vas-tu ? Reviens ici. Vous m'entendez," her mother yelled

Camille didn't look back or respond; she just kept running. She knew a bit of first aid and needed to see if she could help the soldiers. After all, some were only a few years older than her and were fighting for her country. She ran as fast as her little legs would carry her, jumping over cracks and craters in the field. She wasn't worried about her safety. Thankfully, the machine gun crew had abandoned their position, believing a larger number of American soldiers would advance toward them. Their job was to harass the Americans, not to get themselves killed.

With her thoughts on the soldiers, she believed that if she could help just one, then the risk of danger would be worth it. It took her a few minutes to reach the crater's edge. Panting and out of breath, she peered over the rim, then dropped to her knees and cried. She had witnessed death before, many times, but the sheer savagery of the machine gun and artillery was beyond comprehension. After wiping the tears from her eyes, she got up and walked towards the remains of the soldiers. She could do nothing but pray for them. Kneeling, she put her hands together, looked up at the sky, and prayed for their souls.

"Eternal rest grant unto them, O Lord, and let perpetual light shine upon them. May their souls and all the souls of the faithful departed, through the mercy of God, rest in peace. Amen."

As she got up and moved closer, to her right, the man who had shielded his fellow soldier lay partially atop his comrade. His right hand was outstretched, and next to what remained of the brave soldier's hand was a small leather-bound book that resembled a personal diary secured with a rubber band. It was weathered from use but undamaged by the shelling. It was as if it had been placed there by the hand of God. Standing over it, a sense of calm washed over her. Should she pick it up or leave it? She gazed up at the sky and asked God for guidance. As she looked up, the sky darkened, and the rain began to fall. She heard what sounded like a young man's voice. "Pick it up, please, please." She tried to tune the voice out, but it seemed to grow louder. Not a harsh or evil sound, but soothing, more like a young man at peace or an angel.

Camille bent over, picked up the diary, and tucked it into her dress pocket. The voice faded, yet the calmness lingered. The rain stopped, and the clouds parted, revealing a beautiful blue sky. She walked around the other soldiers to see if there was anything she could do for them, even for the one he had attempted to save. They were all dead. Tears streamed down her cheeks. She reached into her pocket and felt the diary. The calmness overtook her once more, and her tears ceased. Today was unlike any other for Camille, as she had thought when she woke up this morning.

Camille ran back home. When she entered the house, her mother had not moved. Camille went up to her bedroom, took out the diary, and tried to read it, but she couldn't understand English and only spoke a few words. The typical phrases were "hello," "goodbye," and "thank you." She placed the diary under her mattress for safekeeping and went downstairs. She wanted to check on her mother. As she entered the kitchen, her mother sat in a chair at the table, the only one remaining out of six. She didn't look up at Camille, resting her head in her hands. She hadn't said a word since Camille got back. Camille felt her mother's pain, but could do nothing. She walked over, wrapped her arms around her mother, and rested her head against hers. She kissed her forehead and said, "I love you, Momma."

She decided to sit at the doorway, hoping an American patrol would come by the house. She needed to inform them about what she had witnessed. Camille didn't want to tell the local authorities; she wasn't sure who she could trust. Years of war turned friends into enemies and once-trusted officials into eyes and ears for the Germans, but she could trust the Americans. After a few hours, a column of soldiers advanced in the distance. Unable to determine their nationality, she waited. As they came closer, she could make out the uniforms. They were American soldiers. Camille got up and ran toward them. As she approached, someone yelled, "Halt, halt." She froze in her tracks, knowing that word in English—it was almost universal.

The column of soldiers stopped, and one of them walked toward her with his pistol aimed at her. Panting from running toward them, she said in French, "American soldiers died over there." She pointed to the field in the distance.

Shaking his head from side to side, the lieutenant replied, "I don't speak French. Do you speak English?" Confused, she answered, "No, no," while pointing toward the dead soldiers. He raised his hand for her to wait. The lieutenant called back to the column, "Get Sergeant Younger up here, double time." Sergeant Edward Younger ran toward Lieutenant Carlson. "Yes, sir."

"You speak French, right? If so, what the hell is she saying? I could make out that it was something about American soldiers."

Sergeant Younger, an average-looking man from Chicago, leaned in and asked, "Pouvez-vous me répéter ce que vous avez dit au lieutenant ici?"

Camille nodded and recounted what she had seen earlier that day. He said, "Reste ici," stood up, glanced at the lieutenant, and shared the story she had just told. "Sergeant, in the field over there?" the lieutenant pointed toward where the soldiers lay.

"Yes, sir. Do you want me to take a couple of men and check it out? It shouldn't take long." After a moment, the lieutenant replied, "Take two men, confirm what she said, and meet us at the T in the road. We'll hold there and wait for you." He pointed north in the direction of the T.

"Yes, sir, the T in the road, two hundred yards north."

The sergeant yelled back to the column, "Circle and Bishop, up here on the double."

Two soldiers broke ranks and ran toward the sergeant. Once they arrived, Sergeant Younger told the girl in French, "Okay, allons-y. Tu ouvres la voie." Camille led the soldiers to the site while the rest continued their mission.

When they reached the crater, Camille pointed and said, "Ils sont là-bas," as she began to cry again.

Sergeant Younger noticed she was visibly disturbed. As an infantry soldier, he had witnessed many deaths, but this was different. He had just returned to his unit after being wounded in combat. Like most soldiers fighting in France, he had only been in the Army for a very short time, joining in February 1917. Since arriving in France, he had participated in the war's most significant battles and had seen his share of combat and its aftermath. He loved the Army but hated war and had lost many friends. He simply wanted it to end so he could move on with his life.

As he peered into the crater, body parts were everywhere, with none of the soldiers' bodies fully intact. He took a deep breath, exhaled, and said, "Come on, we have a mission to complete, and we will complete it." He put his hand on Camille's shoulder. "You stay here," he said to her as the other two soldiers descended into the crater.

Sergeant Younger said, "Hold on, fellas." Then he prayed.

"Merciful and compassionate God, we humbly pray for our deceased soldiers. Remember them in Your endless love and forgive them the sins they may have committed in life. Reward their dedication and selfless service. Comfort and console their grieving loved ones. Amen."

Once he finished the prayer, he turned to his men. "Hey, guys, if their aluminum identification disks are off, put one in a pocket on the body so it can't be lost. If they are still on the bodies, leave with the remains, and bring me the second one. If you find any of their livres, gather them and bring them to me."

Circle and Bishop went in different directions, where the soldiers lay to look for the identity disks and livres and count the bodies. They returned ten minutes later and gave Sergeant Younger the disks and any livres found.

"Hmm, eight disks. That can't be right. I count nine bodies," Sergeant Younger said. "Go back, take another look, and step on it. We need to meet the patrol."

Circle and Bishop conducted a thorough inspection of the crater, searching for the disk or any identification on the remaining body, but they found nothing.

"Sarge, we didn't find anything at all," Private Circle said.

Sergeant Younger walked over to one of the almost fully intact bodies, partially shielding another soldier. A strange feeling came over him. It wasn't fright or fear; a sense of calm filled his heart—a sensation he would never forget. He looked down at the body, knelt, turned it over, and moved the dirt around it, searching for identification tags, but there were none. There was nothing to identify who the soldier was. Unlike the others, half his face was missing.

"Mark the body, and I'll notify the lieutenant. He can take care of it. Come on, let's go." As he started walking away, he turned around and glanced at the carnage. The feeling returned. He turned around, walked out of the crater, and said, "Come on, you two, put some pep in your step."

Both soldiers looked at one another; Bishop whispered, "We were waiting on you."

As they all headed back, Camille said, "I found a diary by one of the bodies. Do you want me to get it for you?"

"Can you describe it to me?" He wanted to see if it was one of the soldiers' livres.

Camille described the diary. It didn't match the livre the American soldier carried, so he said, "No, but I'll let my lieutenant know. If we want it, someone will get it from you. Show me where you live." When they reached the dirt road, she tugged on his shirt sleeve, pointed, and said, "I live in that house."

The sergeant nodded, gave her some of his rations, and walked away. Camille decided that if the Army didn't want it, she would keep the diary and ensure its safekeeping. She hoped that one day, it would find its way home.

A couple of days later, a new unit created out of the Quartermaster Corps, the Grave Registration Service, arrived at the site to document the soldiers' burials. Before burying them, the team did another exhaustive search of the remains and the area, looking for any way to identify the one remaining unknown soldier. Nothing was found. All but one were marked with their names and dates of death. On the lone unknown soldier's gravesite, the marker was inscribed with "Unknown" and the date of his death.

A little over a month later, on November 11th, 1918, the German and Allied powers signed the armistice. It was the first step in ending the four-year-old war that had cost 20,000,000 lives and 21,000,000 wounded. After six months of additional negotiations, the Treaty of Versailles was signed on June 28, 1919, marking the end of the war between Germany and most of the Allied powers.

The War to End All Wars was over. Camille's father returned home a broken, bitter man shortly after the war ended. Consumed by hate, he distanced himself from the family and, in 1920, left without a word, never to return. Her mother passed away soon after—Camille believes it was from a broken heart. Her mom was never the same, and despite Camille's efforts, she could do nothing to help. At seventeen, she became independent, never relying on anyone. Sometimes, she would take out the diary and look over the pages, vowing to learn to read English one day. Even without knowing the words on the pages, she could feel the young soldier's joys, heartache, pain, pride, and loneliness, almost as if he were speaking to her. The remains of the soldier who wrote the diary would be exhumed from his grave, where he died, and relocated to be buried at Meuse-Argonne Cemetery in France, not where he would finally rest. His journey home had only just begun.

CHAPTER 2

HIDE THE DIARY

After the war, Camille moved to Paris to live above a secondhand bookstore. The destruction and memories of her childhood home were too overwhelming for her to bear. Paris would mark the beginning of her life anew.

Initially, finding jobs was challenging. In the years after World War I, unemployment soared in Paris. There was even food rationing, but in 1921, everything shifted. Paris bloomed once more, and the economy thrived. Paris became the epicenter of art, literature, and cinema, thanks to newfound wealth and stability. It was everything Camille had envisioned, the ideal place to move forward with her life. She took a job as a waitress in a café off the Champs-Élysées. She earned enough to live independently and enjoy the nightlife with friends.

Most importantly, she felt safe until September 1, 1939, the day the German army invaded Poland. The peace in Europe was shattered as the continent teetered on the edge of war once again. Twice in her young life, Europe would be engulfed in war. The difference this time was that she would be a fighter in the resistance.

Hitler used the 1919 Treaty that Germany signed in Versailles to launch his war. He believed a war would undo the harsh conditions of the treaty and its effects on the German people.

Before Germany attacked Poland, Hitler aimed to unite all German people under one nation. In 1938, he seized control of a region in Czechoslovakia called the Sudetenland, where over three million Germans resided. On September 1, 1939, Germany invaded Poland, and within thirty-five days, it was under their control. Germany unleashed a blitzkrieg against the Polish people, a strategy they would later apply to their western neighbors. On September 3, France and Britain fulfilled their pledge to Poland and declared war on Germany. Each day, the drumbeats of war grew louder with the invasion of Poland. Germany had its sights set on its neighbors again.

On May 10, 1940, German soldiers invaded France, bringing the war back to Camille. This time, she refused to sit idly by while her country and fellow citizens perished. As the Germans advanced closer to Paris, it seemed they would seize the city within months, if not weeks, just one month after they entered France. The Germans entered Paris on June 14, 1940. After they took control of the city, the café where Camille worked became a favored spot for them to relax and enjoy Paris. It was also an ideal place for an inspiring French resistance operative to operate. The resistance recruited Camille, and she was eager to assist in any way possible. Her memories of World War I were vivid, a wound that would never heal. She couldn't bear to witness her country being ravaged by the Germans once again. With her beauty and friendliness, she quickly became the most sought-after waitress at the café.

German soldiers of all ranks would request Camille when they visited the café. She would eavesdrop on their conversations and relay what she heard to the resistance, which would then give her additional instructions. She continued to document all her discussions with the German soldiers and pass them on to the resistance. She quickly became an integral part of the Paris underground and the fight against the Germans.

In the fall of 1943, three German SS officers were killed by the resistance in a drive-by shooting at a café down the street from where Camille worked. The three officers were also frequent visitors to the café where Camille worked. The Germans' response was quick and vicious. Everyone who worked in the café was arrested, and many of them were executed. However, before they were executed, the Gestapo did what they did best and interrogated the detainees. With the information gathered from the interrogations, the Gestapo visited all the places the SS officers frequented, including Camille's café and other shops and cafés. Shortly after rounding up some of the local resistance, it didn't take long for the Gestapo to narrow their efforts to suspects. They arrested anyone they suspected of being a threat to the occupation of Paris and the German army.

It wasn't long before Camille was on the Gestapo's radar. She worked at the café and had voiced opposition to the German invasion of Poland. One day at work, she was tipped off that the Gestapo was interested in talking to her. It wouldn't be long before they found her and brought her in for interrogation, something she would not let happen. Camille decided it was time to leave Paris as soon as possible.

Camille returned to her apartment that day after work and packed a small backpack with the essentials. She cut and dyed her hair to change her appearance. Her primary goals were to escape Paris and fight the Germans. She couldn't wait any longer and would join up with the French resistance, which was fighting and killing Germans outside of Paris and all over France. She would take the war to the Germans and no longer stand on the sidelines, as she had in the last war. She could sense that she was becoming like her father. There was hate in her heart. She walked over to the dresser and started to take out items she would need. At the bottom of the drawer was her family Bible, which she had taken with her when she left her childhood home, along with the soldier's diary she had found in the artillery crater beside the unknown soldier.

There was no room for either of them, but she couldn't let the Germans find the diary. She wanted to be the one to tell his story. Ideas of what to do with them swirled in her head, but time was running out. Camille took the Bible and opened it to the middle. She took out her knife and cut out the middle pages as tears ran down her cheeks. She was desecrating it, but it was the right thing to do. She knelt and prayed, but the soldier's diary had to be preserved. After the prayer, she got up and continued to cut out the pages where the unknown soldier's words and thoughts would be placed.

When she was done, she wrote a short note and placed it in the front of the diary. Then, she picked up the diary, and a sense of calm overtook her. She felt the same when she picked it up the first time in that field of scorched earth. The hate and rage in her heart were gone for a brief time. She was doing the right thing, but it was a difficult task. She had kept the diary safe for the last twenty or so years. Camille laid the diary in the cut-out pages of her family Bible. Before locking the Bible, she tore out the first page with her family information. She was not going to give the Nazis any idea who owned it in case it was discovered. Once the Bible was closed, she locked it, put it in her backpack, and left her apartment.

The exit from her apartment took her through the secondhand bookstore. She looked around to ensure no one saw her and went to a section in the bookstore near the back wall. After one more look, she pulled some of the books from the shelf and put them on a table beside her. She set her family Bible all the way to the back of the shelf. It was deeper than she thought. Then she returned the books in front to hide the Bible and exited the bookstore through the back entrance, vowing to return for her Bible and the soldier's diary once the war ended.

Camille would never return to Paris. She was killed fighting for the resistance by the Germans in the fall of 1944 in a field, helping a downed American pilot who had just parachuted from his P-38. He was unable to move and was severely burned as the other members of her resistance team assisted the pilot and dragged him to a waiting car. Camille laid down fire to slow the advancing German soldiers. Without any regard for her own life, she continued to fire till she ran out of ammunition. She took out her knife and ran to her left to distract the soldiers.

As she ran, the Germans unleashed a torrent of bullets in her direction, killing her. Her actions allowed the resistance enough time for the pilot to escape and fight another day. The soldier's diary would remain in the bookstore, gathering dust. The soldier's words were lost to the world.

Until one day…

CHAPTER 3

THE BIBLE

As Walter Grover and his son Alex walked past the Delamain bookstore, Alex said, "Hey, Dad, let's go in here." The two had grown apart after a bitter divorce from Alex's mother. He missed the day-to-day conversations with his son, their family vacations, and the feeling of love that came with it. He had a hole in his heart that could only be filled with his son's love. It had been a tough few years, but he was determined to bond with his son, and this vacation to France was the start. They decided to explore Paris in the fall.

After serving twenty years in the Army as a Cavalry Scout (Cav Scout), Walter had retired a few years before. The years away from home and the multiple deployments took a toll on his marriage and family. The years of war took a toll on him, some of the effects visible and others invisible. So, they decided to divorce shortly after he retired. Even though it was a bitter divorce, she continued to support him. There was still a spark of love for him, but he had issues that needed to be resolved. She knew he missed his son. Even though they didn't communicate much, she suggested that he and Alex take a trip as a high school graduation gift. It would give them time together, a great way to bond. She didn't say where. She would leave that up to them.

One Friday night, Walter called Alex and asked him to take a European trip as a graduation gift. Even after the divorce, he would still take his ex-wife's advice, which he couldn't explain. Alex discussed it with his mother, and of course, she agreed. It was her idea. The following week, they were in France.

They had just arrived in Paris the day before. The jet lag was kicking their butts, but they were determined to explore Paris and the surrounding areas. They only had a few days left of their vacation.

As they walked down the busy Rue Saint-Honoré, Alex saw a shop he wanted to explore. Walter watched as Alex veered toward the store.

"Alex, really, a secondhand bookstore?"

"No, forget it. Never mind, Dad," Alex replied.

"No, no. I'm just surprised. Let's go in." There was excitement in his voice.

Alex opened the door and held it open for his dad. As Alex entered, a feeling came over him. He felt calm and relaxed, a sense he hadn't felt in a long time. It seemed the time he spent with his dad was always stressful. He couldn't explain why, but since the divorce, he felt stressed when his mom dropped him off at his dad's. He loved his dad, but expressing it was hard for him. He agreed to the vacation in an attempt to bond before it was past the point of no return. He wanted his dad in his life, but they were both hard-headed and stubborn.

As his dad explored the front section of the bookstore, Alex felt drawn to the back, strolling along the shelves of vintage books. Occasionally, he would pull a book out, thumb through it, and then return it to the shelf. He went deeper into the store. The farther he got, the dustier the books got. He continued exploring until he passed a bookshelf that gave him a calming feeling. Then, hair raised on his neck. He stopped and backed up, and the feeling decreased. He straightened up, and the sensation grew. He looked to his left and pulled out a very old Le Comte de Monte-Cristo edition. The feeling increased. He put the book down, stood on his tiptoes, and saw another book against the wall. He grabbed it. It was cumbersome, but he managed to pull it out and look at it. The black book had no title. However, on the binding was inscribed "La Sainte Bible."

Alex whispered to himself, "Hmm, a Bible."

As he held it in his hands, a feeling rose inside him. Alex was not religious. He didn't regularly attend church, but he was a believer. Unable to describe the feeling, he stared at the Bible again and decided to put it back, placing the copy of Le Comte de Monte-Cristo in front of it as he had found it. After all, what would he do with a Bible in French? Plus, it had a lock. He looked around for the key, but there was no key to be found. As he put it back, the feeling subsided.

He stepped away but was drawn back. Standing by the bookshelf, he heard his father.

"Alex, are you ready to go?"

He turned to his right, stopped, took out the copy of Le Comte de Monte-Cristo, took out the Bible, and walked toward his dad.

"Hey, Dad, look what I found."

"A Bible. Nice. Now, let's go."

"I want to buy it, please."

Walter saw something in his son's face he hadn't seen in years. He looked peaceful and excited at the same time. "Let me check it out first."

Alex gave him the Bible. "Son, there's a lock on it. Are you sure you want it?"

"Yes. You can open it. I have faith in you."

A smile came over Walter's face. His son hadn't said that to him in years. "Well, it is pretty cool. Okay, let's get it."

Alex leaned into his dad and whispered, "Do you feel it?"

He turned his head, frowning. "Feel what? It's heavy for sure."

"No, no. I can't explain it, Dad."

"Hungry?"

They both laughed. "Must be the jet lag, and well, I'm hungry, but that's not it. So, can we still get it?"

"Sure, let's get it. It's pretty cool. I wonder how old it is."

They walked up to the counter to pay. Walter said in his best French, "How much is this? We'd like to buy it."

The young clerk looked up and replied, "I speak English, but thanks for trying. Americans rarely attempt to speak French. Let me see how much this is." She took the Bible and turned it over. There was no price sticker. "Hmm, interesting. It doesn't have a price. I'm not sure how much to charge. Where did you get it? What section?"

Alex pointed to the back.

"Hmm, I have never seen this before, and I just went through that section," she said.

The owner was not at the store, so she couldn't ask her. She smiled at Alex and asked, "How about twenty euros?"

"Well, that sounds a little low, but great. We'll take it." Walter took out his wallet and gave her a twenty-euro note.

She handed them the Bible back in a cloth bag. "Have a great time in Paris."

They left the bookstore and headed to get lunch. The excitement Alex felt was almost palpable. He had a little extra pep in his step.

CAFÉ PLUME: PARIS, FRANCE

After leaving Delamain bookstore, they stopped in a little café down the street called Café Plume. They sat outside, facing the Rue Saint-Honoré across the street from the Louvre Museum.

"Dad, thanks for buying the Bible. It's so cool. I can't wait until we can open it," Alex said.

"You're welcome. So, why the sudden interest in this Bible?"

"I don't know." Alex glanced at the book on the table. "Have you ever felt something draw you to it?"

"I can't say I have, but I get it. I'm looking forward to opening it. I wonder how old it is? It looks pretty old."

As they talked, a waitress came to the table. "Que désirez-vous?"

"Hey, Dad, let me try." Alex faced the waitress. "Deux cafés et deux salads et frites."

She looked at him and said in perfect English, "Damn, that was pretty good. Two coffees and salads with noodles."

Alex stared at her. "Noodles?"

She laughed and put her hand on his shoulder. "I'm just messing with you two. French fries coming up."

Walter looked over to his son and asked, "Coffee? When did you start drinking coffee?

"Well, Dad, I thought, when in Paris, do as a Parisian."

Walter smiled and replied, "This I have to see."

"While they waited for their food, they sat back and enjoyed the view of Paris. Alex leaned into the table and said, "Dad, thanks for taking me to Paris. I really like it. I know it's been hard for both of us, but I want to thank you."

His dad put his hands on the table. "I wouldn't want to be anywhere else with anyone else, son. I love you."

They sat there, enjoying the moment. It wasn't long before the waitress returned with their lunch. She set the plates on the table and asked, "Where did you learn French?"

"I took a couple of years in school," Alex said. "Sorry if I butchered it."

"No, no. It was perfect. Enjoy your salads and French fries. Let me know when you're ready to leave."

Alex picked up his cup of coffee and took a sip. The look on his face said it all. Walter asked the waitress, "Can you please bring a Coke?"

She replied, chuckling, "Yes, of course."

"Thanks, Dad."

Within a minute or two, the waitress brought the Coke and placed it in front of Alex.

"We can pay now if that's better," Walter said.

"Yes, of course, I will be right back with the bill."

She returned and laid the check on the table. Once it was paid, they finished their lunch, got up, and headed for the hotel.

MARRIOTT HOTEL: PARIS, FRANCE

In their room, they sat at the small round table in the center. Alex took the Bible from the bag and placed it on the table. He moved his hands over the Bible's cover. He could feel the texture and stitching. His father took out his Swiss Army knife and attempted to pop the lock. With the calm hand of a watchmaker, he placed the knife blade under the top portion of the lock and slowly twisted, being careful not to cut or damage the lock or the Bible. After a few minutes, the Bible was unlocked.

Alex looked at his dad and smiled. He got up and hugged him. "Damn, Dad, that was pretty cool."

"Hey, I was in the Army at one time."

Alex sat back down. "Can I open it first?"

"Hell, yes, go for it."

Alex opened the Bible as his dad got up and walked over to the window. "Thank you, God."

"Did you say something?" Alex asked.

"No, just looking outside."

Alex lifted the book's cover. The first page, where the family information should be, was missing. It appeared to have been torn out in haste. The next page displayed the title and other information about the book in French, which he couldn't read. But there was one thing he could read: the Bible, which was printed in 1880.

He did a quick calculation in his head. "Wow, it's over 140 years old. Damn." He turned the pages, intent on looking at each and every one. Even though he may not be able to read the text, he could see that the drawings and colored maps were beautiful. He stopped before halfway and said, "Dad, check this out." He lifted it slightly to show him one of the colorful maps of the holy land.

His father sat back down and peered at Alex. "Wow, the color has not faded, but you can tell the book has been well read. Amazing." It was obvious that Alex was mesmerized by the Bible, so he decided to go and lie down and leave him to examine it. The jet lag was getting to him. "Hey, son, I'm going to take a quick nap. Wake me up when you want to go."

"Okay, Dad. Man, this bible is amazing."

As Alex studied each page, he was amazed by the artwork, maps, and the beauty of the writing.

Walter had been asleep for almost an hour when he heard, "Dad, Dad, wake up, wake up."

Startled, he got up and said, "Alex, what is it? What's going on?"

With more excitement, Alex said, "There's a book hidden in the Bible."

His mind was still foggy from being asleep, so he replied, "What? A book hidden in the Bible?

He rolled out of bed and walked over to the table. A leather diary lay in the middle of the Bible, cut out to make room for it. By the looks of it, this diary had been hidden from the world for over eighty years.

"Dad, what should I do? Can I take it out?" Alex asked.

"Wait. Was there any identification in the Bible? Like, whose was it?"

"No, nothing." Alex showed him the first page, where the family tree or information was torn out. "See? Whoever this belonged to, they didn't want anyone to know." Alex turned back to where the diary was lying. "Dad, can I take it out?"

His father nodded.

With shaking hands, he pulled the diary out of its hiding place. Those feelings in the bookstore returned when he touched the diary, but now they were more intense. It was like he could feel the emotions in the pages of the diary. He released the diary, stared at his dad, and then closed the Bible.

"Son, you're white as a sheet. Are you okay?"

"Yes, I think so. I can't explain it. I felt the same way in the bookstore, but this time, there were emotions in the diary. Nothing scary, hell, I can't explain it."

"Do you want to take it back to the bookstore?"

"Oh no, I want to read it. I think it wants me to read it. Crazy, but it wants to be read."

Alex opened the Bible and turned to where the diary lay. This time, his hands weren't shaking. He put his fingers around the diary and gently pulled it out of its hiding place for the first time in over eighty years—but they didn't know that.

He couldn't believe its condition as it looked almost new.

He placed it on the table. "Well, here goes, Dad."

CHAPTER 4

OFF TO WAR

With the diary in his hands, Alex sat at the table and opened it. Inside the diary was a handwritten note. The note was in French, and Alex translated as best he could.

"I found this diary next to the remains of a U.S. soldier near my hometown on the banks of the Aire River. Machine gun fire and an artillery barrage killed him and his fellow soldiers in October 1918. He died trying to protect his soldiers. He is a hero."

Walter said, "Son, can I see the note, please?"

He took the note and read it to himself. When he was done, he handed it back. Rubbing his chin, he said, "Here, put the note back where you found it."

Alex took the note, placed it back in the diary, and closed it. "Dad, I want to read this like a book and not jump around. I want to get to know the soldier as I believe that's how he intended it to be read."

"I couldn't agree with you more. Are you going to read it out loud?"

"You know what, yes, I think so."

Carefully, he opened the diary and scanned the first page. He couldn't believe its condition. The pages were not torn, brittle, or weathered. Every word was legible. He leaned forward and began to read, then stopped. "Dad, I'm going to read the date first, then what's written underneath it. If there is no date, I will just read his words."

He started on the first page ...

READY TO BOARD - JUNE 1917

"We arrived near where we will board the ships after our long journey from our posts. I counted at least three huge ships at the dock. Everyone looks so spiffy in our new uniforms. Last night, we stopped for the night and then marched in this morning during the darkness. Kinda eerie. The streets were almost empty to the piers, but a few folks were still out, waving at us. It's nice to see all the people out in the streets cheering us. We were told not to tell anyone where we were going, but somehow, I think these good people know.

We waited a day to board the ship. It has been a busy couple of months. Everyone is upbeat. It's like we are all going on a vacation. Everyone's face was the same: excitement, pride, and uncertainty. I heard my platoon sergeant telling us to get in formation. It's almost time to board. I was a little nervous! All the units had to fit on these ships. The ships are enormous. I have never been on a boat other than the rowboats we would put in the lake. I wonder how it even floated. It was so massive. They are enormous! I wondered if they would fit everyone on them. When we got ours, I thought, hell, you could get lost in it. We were told where to go; heck, I just followed my squad leader. Well, they fit my entire unit on this one ship. Luckily, all my company is in the same section of the vessel. It's cramped, to say the least. I hope we won't be on this thing long."

1ST DAY AT SEA

"We started to sea but got as far as a harbor and stayed there a couple of days. They wanted us to get used to living on a ship. I can tell you, I'm not. I don't really believe it was to get us used to living on the ship. I believe the

Navy ensured that there were no enemy submarines nearby. But I'm just a private and don't know crap, and I have learned in my short time in the Army, it's hurry up and wait.

Once we started the journey, we were not alone. There were a few Navy warships with us that I could see. I'm pretty sure I didn't see them all, and I don't want to say precisely how many are with our convoy. It's one thing the Army teaches, which is to keep your mouth shut. I'm unsure how long we'll sail or where we're going, but today is the day. The weather was excellent, warm and sunny, but not as hot as where we came from. It looked like it might be cramped where we are going to bunk. We were all assigned a spot in our section, which was located in the middle of the ship, a few decks below the main deck. Like me, most of us didn't like being in the middle of the ship, but there was nothing we could do. We are just soldiers. It was not a place where I felt comfortable. There were more soldiers together in one place than I had ever seen. We are excited, a feeling in the air I can't explain. Everyone was in a joyous mood. It was contagious. We are as well-trained, or at least we think we are, and we are ready to enter the war.

We sailed past the Statue of Liberty to the open sea. Wow, what a sight! By seeing her, I know in my heart that we are all doing the right thing. The harbor's calm waters were gone when we reached the open sea. So far, I have spent most of my time on the top deck. The ocean has been rough. The waves are enormous. I'm sure glad I didn't join the Navy. My stomach has been messed up. It's hard to keep something down, seasick! Yes, I guess there is such a thing."

2ND DAY AT SEA

"I'm feeling a lot better. I haven't eaten much. I want to make sure I can keep what I eat down—the day started with physical training. With little in my stomach, it was a challenge to complete all the exercises, as I didn't have much energy. We must be in shape when we arrive in Europe so that I can give it one hundred percent. Plus, I want to look good for the ladies. I'm just kidding. You are the only one for me, and you have been since the day I met you. There are rumors of German U-boats in the area, and the sailors manning the weapons are constantly practicing and shooting at targets. I

have to say, I'm glad they are practicing. They need it. I bet a couple of bucks on one of them and lost. He didn't hit one of his targets."

5TH DAY AT SEA

"I can keep my food down, and honestly, the chow is pretty good. I enjoy going to the top deck and watching the sailors practice firing their weapons. I got to fire one of their machine guns. Now that was fun! Hitting the targets is harder than it looks in the open ocean, as they move up and down with the waves. We practiced abandoning the ship. I think it would be chaos if we had to abandon the ship. A man won't last long in the cold waters of the North Atlantic. So far, no sightings of German subs."

6TH DAY AT SEA

"Happy birthday, our first one apart. I spent the day cleaning equipment and helping out the platoon sergeant. He needed a couple of soldiers to help transport some of the supplies we would need when we arrived in France. It only took a couple of hours, but it was good to do something different. I hope your day was great. I can't wait until I'm home and we can spend it together."

10TH DAY AT SEA

"I haven't written much, and there is not a lot to tell. We still do physical training every morning, but now we are working with our weapons. The sailors are getting a little better and hitting their targets. Still, thank God, there have been no submarine sightings.

I was on the top deck last night. The weather was perfect—the water was like glass. I could see the reflection of the sky in the water. It was like looking into a mirror. The sky was crystal clear. I decided to take in the view before going to the lower deck for bed. I lay down and looked at the stars. My god, the sky was pitch black and full of them. There must have been a million, maybe more. I could see the Big Dipper, Little Dipper, and Orion's Belt. It's peaceful out here in the middle of the North Atlantic Ocean, but I know there is danger. The Navy wouldn't send ships to protect us if there were no danger.

A man can do a lot of thinking out here. When we aren't doing Army stuff, my buddies and I talk about how we are going to single-handedly win the war and kill as many Germans as we can in doing so. End the war in record time, maybe before winter. One of the guys in the platoon said he had visited Paris before the war, and the women were beautiful. The funny part is that he tried to talk with a French accent. Needless to say, he needed to work on it. But he does speak a little French. If you don't think that riled everyone up, talking about beautiful French women, you have no idea. Talking like that when he knows there is not a single woman within a thousand miles of us. I only have eyes for you. Everyone, including me, can't wait to get to Paris, but not the girls. The faster we get there, the quicker the war ends, and I'll be home. We also talk about what we will do when the war is over. Hell, I know that is crazy. We haven't even got there yet. It helps pass the time. I heard we only have three days until we get to where we got off this thing. I can't wait."

DAY 12: FINAL DAY AT SEA

"At four a.m. this morning, everyone woke up to the voice of our platoon sergeant yelling, 'Get your asses up and get your gear squared away. We are leaving this ship today; formation is scheduled for 9 a.m. on the top deck. Your ass better be ready and have all your gear, and don't forget your damn rifle." Damn, I'm glad he got us up. I need to repack a lot of my gear. Pulling things out here and there, luckily, looking around, I'm not the only one.

Later in the day, a soldier who had been on the deck ran into our section and said, 'A sailor told him. We should be able to see the coast in the next couple of hours.'

After packing all my gear, I rushed to the top deck and took a quick look. I could see the coast but didn't know where we would disembark. I went back down to the hold and told everyone. They all moved a little faster, even the soldiers who were slow getting their gear together. It's remarkable how small things can motivate someone. I'm glad I didn't have to do anything but wait for the orders to move to the top deck to disembark. After a couple of hours, we will be off this thing. I'm ready!

The orders came down to move to the top deck, and we did it with a purpose. As we made our way to the top deck, one of the soldiers said, 'The coast of France is right over there,' pointing to his right. We could see the coast of France, what a beautiful sight! Everyone went wild. The joy of knowing the journey was almost over was beyond words. The faces of the soldiers spoke volumes. Everyone on the ship has aged. It wouldn't be long before we were on French soil and getting into the fight. At least, that is what we hope. For many of us, the realization of going to war was very real."

Alex stopped reading, looked at his dad, and said, "I feel like I'm almost there with him. Hey, Dad, can you please look up when the first American soldiers left for World War I? Oh, and before I forget, where did they get off the ship?"

It took a few minutes before his father said, "I got the information. Damn, the internet is good. The first troops departed Hoboken, New Jersey, for France on June 10th and disembarked at Port de Saint-Nazaire, France, on June 26th. Here, look, I googled it." He looked up. "Come on, son, let's get something to eat and see the lights of Paris. We can read some more in the morning."

"Dad, just a couple more pages, please."

"Well, it's early, so sure, go for it. But only a few more. I'm getting hungry." He smiled.

TRAINING CAMP: NEAR SAINT-NAZAIRE, FRANCE

JUNE 26TH, 1917

"Well, we made it off the ship. I couldn't believe how wobbly my legs were, and I felt, well, not dizzy, but like I was walking on waves. It's hard to explain. I asked one of the sailors, and he said, 'I must have gotten my sea legs.' I replied that I needed my marching legs, shook his hand, and said 'Thank you.' I know he is in as much danger as I'm about to get in. We spoke

a little prayer together before parting ways. I didn't want to be late for my formation.

We marched through the town. There were a few folks who lined the streets to get their first glimpse of U.S. soldiers. We all felt a renewed sense of pride. We marched with our heads held high and our shoulders back.

My unit and I have arrived at our new home away from home. It's not bad, it's just outside of town. It's close enough to see it, but far enough that we know we won't visit anytime soon. There is a lot of training that must be done. As we arrived, there was little fanfare. I think they were surprised to see us Americans. As we walked through the streets, it was hard to imagine a war happening just miles from us—the houses were so different from home and much older. As we marched past the buildings, I could read the year some of them were built. One had 1807, over one hundred years old. When we arrived at camp, we were assigned to a building. It looks like they put them up last night. The construction is not the best. But it keeps us out of the weather, which is beautiful. Once we got into the building, the rest of the platoon and I put our gear away. We had a formation within ten minutes after stowing our gear. We had drills and training to do. After all, we need to prepare for the Germans.

The platoon sergeant informed us that taps were at 9 p.m. and the reveille at 4 a.m. The first formation would be at 6 a.m. It must be nine; I heard taps, it was to hit the hay. I'm beat."

June 27th, 1917

"Well, like a well-oiled machine, the bugler played reveille at four. Shortly after reveille, I heard the loud voice of my platoon sergeant. 'Assess up. Come on, boys, we have a war to fight.' I jumped out of bed, and I must say, I slept great last night. My makeshift bed was comfortable. There was time for latrine and chow before formation.

During the formation, the platoon leader and the platoon sergeant briefed us on the camp and what we could expect to encounter. They told us where we could go and where we couldn't, and the chow hours. For the first couple of weeks, it's all about physical conditioning. The platoon sergeant handed out the training schedule for the day. With everyone still assembled, the color guard hoisted the U.S. flag over the camp. As the flag was raised, the band played the Star-Spangled Banner. With the flag fluttering in the wind, the stars and stripes were magnificent. Everyone felt a renewed sense of patriotism as they heard the music and saw the flag waving. Before you ask, yes, we have a band.

While we were setting up camp this afternoon, the sun warmed up the inside of the building. Thank God there was a light breeze. It's hot in our uniforms. We have to keep them buttoned up all the time.

We didn't get much time for ourselves. We are going to spend the next couple of weeks unloading equipment and setting up the camp, and I've heard we'll be getting in tip-top shape. Well, that's it for today. I'm exhausted. It's been a long day. Tomorrow should be interesting. You're in my thoughts."

JUNE 28TH, 1917

"Another great night's sleep. Like every day on the ship since our platoon sergeant woke us up at 4 a.m. the first morning. I got up, got dressed, and ate breakfast. Not much to talk about, but damn, I was starving. After breakfast, we had our 6 a.m. formation, where our Commanding Officer, a captain, came out and gave a brief speech. This is what I remember he said:

'Soldiers, we are here for one reason. To fight and defeat the Germans. But to do that and win, we must train, be in the best physical shape possible, and hone our war-fighting skills. The training will be as realistic as possible, and it will be tough. Our French allies will be leading most of the training. They have the experience and will teach us everything they know. We will teach them that we are Americans, and we will fight with all our might, never giving up. We don't complain. We execute our missions with all our being. We fight as a unit but can think as individuals. To accomplish these tasks today, we will begin with a ten-mile march carrying full backpacks at 9 a.m. Once we get done with the march, we will practice bayonet training with our French comrades. After that, if any time remains, your platoon sergeants will provide the rest of the day's training schedule. Everyone will always wear their uniform correctly, and all buttons will be fastened. No excuses and no exceptions. We will not be a rag-tag group. You will conduct yourselves as such. You will always display military courtesy to our allies. You will show

respect to the French population. We are American-fighting men. To the French and British, we are the United States and will represent ourselves and fight as one. We will not show weakness but courage in the face of the enemy. We are soldiers, and we are fighting for a just cause. You will hear one central theme as you talk to the French and British soldiers. The Germans are a very formidable fighting force, but can be defeated and will be.' He ended his speech with, 'Don't get too comfortable here; we won't be here long.'

As he was talking, I looked around the unit and saw in the young men's faces a look I hadn't seen before, and some of these guys I had known for months. It finally hit home. We are going to war, and some of us won't survive. Oh, well, we must get ready to fight, but first, we have a lot of marching to do. I miss you!"

JUNE 29TH, 1917

"I peeled potatoes for hours and hours. There must have been thousands. I had KP duty (Kitchen Police) today, which got me out of marching for a day and gave me extra chow. The mess sergeant was tough, but he took care of me as long as I did what he said. KP made for an extremely long day."

JULY 1ST, 1917

"They weren't kidding about getting in shape. Yesterday, we did a twenty-mile march with full backpacks and a full combat load. My legs are killing me. The blisters on my feet have blisters of their own. Some guys couldn't make it, so they are marching again today. None in my platoon fell out of the march. We all made it. We had some personal time today to clean gear and relax a little. I'm taking care of my blisters. The weather has been great. The sun has been shining and warm, but not hot. The trees have beautiful leaves, the flowers bloom, and the bees buzz. A charming place if not for the war."

JULY 5TH, 1917

"I can't believe I made it to Paris on the 4th of July. My god, the city is fantastic from what little I saw. A few units were selected to participate in a

parade and march down the Champs-Élysées. We stared at the Place De La Concorde up to the tomb of Lafayette Arc. As we approached the Arc De Triomphe, I could see the Eiffel Tower in the distance. Even from a distance, it was impressive. Hell, the whole city was alive. As we marched, the citizens of Paris showed up in full force. They lined the streets, one side and the other, in groups on balconies, some even standing on housetops. They were wildly enthusiastic. They were yelling Sammies, Yankees, or Teddies. I guess those are the nicknames they have given us. Shoot, I have been called worse. But I felt so proud. I couldn't believe we were the first American soldiers to leave the United States to fight a war in Europe and, I hope, the last. They call this a world war, meaning so many countries are fighting. I have heard of some on the German side, such as Austria and Hungary, as well as some other countries I have never heard of, like Bulgaria. They call them the Central Powers. I have no idea why. On our side, the allies include the French, British, Italians, Belgians, Japanese, and a few more. They call this the war to end all wars.

Heck, all of us had smiles on our faces. Remember when the soldier on the ship said the women of France are beautiful? Well, he wasn't lying; they are. However, you, my dear, are the most beautiful and the only one who has my heart.

The French even had an airplane fly over and do acrobatics. They went all out. We won't let them down. As we made our way through the crowds, we encountered French soldiers on leave; most of them appeared to have just returned from the front. Some even had bandages on their heads and arms in slings; some were missing a leg or an arm. I saw in their faces a look I had never seen in any human being. I can't explain it other than as a feeling of emptiness and despair. I think the best word to describe it would be melancholy. However, I could still sense pride and a sense of patriotism. If needed, they would all return to the fight. I'm sure the less severely wounded would be. I know for me, at least, it kinda took the joy out of the parade. I knew then we were going to war, and there was going to be a cost in human lives and limbs.

As we continued to march, flowers were thrown at us from the streets and the rooftops, like leaves falling from a tree in the fall. Heck, some of us put them in the barrel of our rifle or our belt. It looked like a field of marching flowers, so beautiful and peaceful. Wave after wave of colored flowers move across a field of grass. That was the picture I had in my head. The bright colors of the flower petals against our cold steel rifle barrels were like a contrast in times—one of joy and celebration, and the other of upcoming death.

After the parade, we didn't spend much time in the city, but we did get a little time to walk around. A group of us went to the Eiffel Tower. In the distance, it looked amazing, but standing next to it would take your breath away. After that, we walked back down toward the Louvre Museum. I spotted a small bookstore and decided to stop by. It was called Libraire Delamain, and the clerks said it was the oldest in Paris. I told my buddies I would write a book one day, and it would be in the store. At the same time, they all replied, 'Sure, after the war, we will all buy one.'"

"Stop," his dad said. "What did you say? Read that again."

"From where?"

"The part around the bookstore."

"After that, we walked back down toward the Louvre Museum. I spotted a small bookstore and decided to stop by. It was called Libraire Delamain, and the clerks said it was the oldest in Paris. I told my buddies I would write a book one day, and it would be in the store."

"Do you remember the name of the bookstore from which we bought the Bible? The Delamain."

Alex was silent for a bit, then said, "Damn—sorry, Dad—but wow, that's crazy, right?"

"To say the least, it's quite the coincidence. Hey, Alex, how about we retrace the steps he took in the parade tomorrow?"

"Dad, now that sounds like a plan. Let's go and eat. I'm starving."

CHAPTER 5

PREPARING FOR WAR

Alex woke up and peered out the window to check the weather. It was a beautiful, sunny fall day. He was ready to start retracing the soldier's steps, and it looked like a perfect day to be outside. He strolled over to his dad's bed and said, "Come on, Dad, get up, let's go. We have a lot of ground to cover today."

Walter opened one eye. "What time is it?"

Alex glanced at his watch. "It's seven."

"Seven? We're on vacation. We can sleep in."

"Not today. Today, we are going marching." He laughed.

Getting out of bed, Walter said, "No marching for me, son, I have done my fair share."

Alex stood at attention, saluted, and said, "Yes, sir."

"Hey, I work for a living. Let me get dressed."

As his dad got cleaned up and dressed, Alex sat back in a chair and thought about what he had read the previous day. The words had come alive, and when he closed his eyes, he could see them play out in his head like a movie.

After a few minutes, his dad exited the bathroom, ready to go.

Alex picked up the diary and put it in his backpack. "I'm going to cut you some slack. We can eat before we start this journey."

"Well, thank you, sir," his dad said.

"No problem, Sergeant."

His dad just looked at him and smiled. It had been years since he had called him sergeant, and memories returned to him. Alex would always greet him when he arrived home from a deployment with, "Welcome home, Sergeant. I missed you, Daddy." To Walter, this was a sign of respect.

They left the hotel room and took the elevator to the lobby.

They took the short walk to the parade route and occasionally stopped to reflect on the diary's contents. After walking the route, they stopped at a café for lunch near Place de la Concorde, one of the major squares in Paris. They could see the Luxor Obelisk towering more than seventy-five feet in the air as they sat there. After eating lunch, they walked over to a park bench on a path lined with plane trees. Their brightly colored leaves had already changed for fall, and the onslaught of winter was right around the corner.

While sitting in the sun, Alex took the diary out of his backpack and read it aloud, while Walter sat there, enjoying the time he spent with his son.

UNIT CAMP: CENTRAL FRANCE

July 9th, 1917

"The day after the parade, we loaded up and moved to a new location. Sorry, I can't say where. The most memorable part of the two-day journey was the train ride—nothing like the ride from our posts in the States. We were loaded like cattle in the train cars. 'I called them cattle cars.' It seemed to stick. The entire unit started calling them cattle cars. But at least we made it safe and sound. After seeing the airplane do its acrobatics, I am glad we didn't get attacked from the air. There would have been nowhere to run or hide.

We are all housed in an old barn, which hasn't been used in years. There were cobwebs everywhere. Well, it's been a hell of a journey—it's time to hit the hay. In my wooden bed, with a very thin mattress and a couple of blankets. I think hay might be more comfortable. I'm not sure I will use them since it's so hot, and there is not a lot of air circulating through the building. I'm going to use one of the blankets to make a pillow. Maybe one day we can have a farm. I promise we won't have to sleep in the barn."

July 10th, 1917

"We started our training today. Although we have basic soldiering skills, we continue to undergo additional individual training. According to the platoon sergeant, there will be three phases of training, each lasting approximately a month, and we are currently in the first phase. We started the day with a march out to the firing range. I have never fired so many rounds. My rifle jammed twice, but I could clear it and continue firing. I spent most of the time on the range, firing from mock trenches and on my belly. That was the fun part of the morning. The not-so-fun part was that we had to pick up all the brass casings from the bullets.

Once we finished on the range, we ate our rations. I had corned beef and hard bread, and washed it all down with water. By the time I get home, I'm sure I will not eat one bite of corned beef, but it's darn good right now. After lunch, we moved to the bayonet range. Just the thought of having to stab someone with my bayonet turns my stomach. But if it comes to that, I will do it. It's either him or me. I have a lot of living to do. The French instructors demonstrated the best technique for the quickest kill. What at one time I thought was easy, attaching the bayonet to my rifle, became increasingly more difficult with someone yelling in my ear and someone charging at me. Some soldiers dropped their bayonets on the ground, and the French instructors would stop the training and say, 'You're one man down. This soldier is dead! This must become second nature, with no hesitation. Your life and those of your fellow soldiers depend on it.' We must have done this for hours, or it seemed like it had been hours. Once everyone had completed the task, we marched back to the barracks.

Well, I need to clean my rifle and get ready for tomorrow. You are in my dreams."

JULY 12TH, 1917

"What a day! I got to throw some hand grenades. You pull the pin, release the spoon, and throw it. It's not like throwing a baseball, but it's about straightening your arm back and bringing it forward. It's not the way I learned to throw a baseball. Luckily, we had time to practice with dummy ones. Hell, one of the guys froze with a live one. The French sergeant grabbed it out of his hand and threw it. You would think they would make him leave the pit, but nope. They made him throw three more, but he didn't freeze again. I hope to be as calm as the sergeant when the time comes. Once everyone was done with the grenades, we immediately transitioned into hand-to-hand combat and learned how to fight with our trench knives. By the end of the day, I had a nice cut on my arm, but it was not too bad. I just put a bandage over it and kept going.

We all went down to a small river that runs by our camp and got cleaned up. It was pretty relaxing. The sun was out, and it was hot. The cool water felt so good. I didn't get as clean as a bath, but I got to wash off some of the dirt. Heck, I still had most of my clothes on, so I washed up and cleaned my uniform. Within minutes, both sides of this small river were filled with soldiers wanting to wash up. But you know, when you get a bunch of men together, it didn't take long before we shoved each other in the water. We laughed like we hadn't laughed since we got here. It's the small, insignificant things in life that matter. Well, after a few minutes, the first sergeant broke up the fun. Well, at least we got somewhat clean."

JULY 15TH, 1917

"Today was gas day. I had to wear the M1 gas mask for almost the entire day. I hate it. It feels so confining, but I know I have to wear it when we get hit with a gas attack, which we will. It will save my life. Our instructor, a French sergeant, was the victim of a gas attack. His voice sounded very raspy. He said it was from mustard gas and was lucky to be alive. Usually, when you're exposed to mustard, it will kill you within weeks, a horrible, agonizing death.

We got hit with a simulated gas attack. The warning gongs and bells could be heard. Since we might be with the British army, they demonstrated their warning device, a rattle. You hold it and spin it around. Once the alarm was sounded, we had only seconds to put on our masks. Those who didn't have to redo the drill until the task was accomplished within nine seconds. I only had to do it three times. Once we passed the task, they had us walk through some gas to show us how the mask works, then run from there to the formation.

The crazy part is when we entered the gas cloud; they made us take off our masks, take a deep breath, put them back on, and seal them. The one sergeant said, 'It was to build confidence in the mask and to demonstrate it does work.' It was a sight to see. Stuff was coming out of soldiers' noses and mouths. One thing they said before we went into the gas cloud was, 'Don't rub your eyes after taking off your mask.' Well, some of them either didn't hear or pay attention. I saw a couple of soldiers rub their eyes after removing their masks, and they couldn't see for a few minutes. I went over to one of them, and all you could see was the white part of his eyes. It was like their eyes rolled back. They had to have their eyes washed out with water. Once they could see, they made them redo the task. They didn't rub them again. It only takes one time to sink in.

It was hard enough to run before taking it off and putting it back on, but after breathing in whatever it was, it was tough to breathe with it on. We were told to run to the firing range while waiting to complete the gas exercise. What seemed like miles was only fifty yards to a firing line on the range. There, we had to fire our weapons. Usually, I'm an excellent shot, but wearing the mask is more like aiming and firing and hoping to hit something or someone. My mask gets fogged up when I'm breathing fast and hard. Once we got the all-clear sign, we removed our masks. Sweat came pouring out of my mask, along with everyone else's. I took a big gulp of air.

One of the soldiers asked what happens if you don't have your gas mask with you. The reply came quickly and sternly. 'You'd better have your gas mask with you all the time. Even when you're taking a crap, is that understood? From now on, it's part of your uniform. Just like your helmet.' They showed us what looked like a giant cotton bandage soaked in water that could be used in case you couldn't reach your gas mask. I think I will keep my mask with me. I'm not sure that a cotton bandage will have any effect. I don't have a lot of confidence in the cotton bandage."

July 16th, 1917

"Today, we started to work as an infantry squad, and one of the guys was promoted to corporal. He will make a good leader. We started learning to communicate without saying a word. We used hand signals and chirps from a whistle. By the end of the day, the corporal could move the entire squad from one location to another without making a sound. They taught us different formations for movement, such as the column, wedge, and line. Tomorrow, we will review movement within the squads, based on what they said, and how we will approach the Germans. A frontal attack."

PARK BENCH: PARIS, FRANCE

Alex stopped reading and closed the diary. "Hey, Dad, do you know hand signals?"

"Hell, yes," he replied.

"Okay, show me, soldier. Come on, Dad."

Walter got up off the bench. "The first one I'm going to show you is how to move out. Now, when I put my right arm up and move it forward, it means to move out and start walking." He moved his right arm forward.

"Cool. Okay, a couple more, please."

"When I put my hand down, that means you get on the ground. When I put my right arm up, that means stop."

Alex gave his dad a high-five. "Not bad, soldier."

"Okay, I have one more, but it's not really a recognized hand signal. Do you want to see it?"

"Are you kidding me? Heck, yes."

"Okay, here goes. Now, you can do this with either the left or the right hand. I will do it with my right hand. Come on, do it with me. Put your right hand out, palm facing down. Take your left middle finger like you're flipping someone off. Now, tap your palm with the middle finger. By the way, don't flip anyone off."

Alex laughed. "Okay, I think this one is BS. What does it mean?"

Walter, laughing, replied, "Cover me. I'm getting screwed."

They were both laughing when Alex asked, "Dad, screwed is not the word you used in the Army, was it?"

"No," he replied. They kept laughing. Walter was in heaven.

They sat back down, and Walter looked at his watch. "How about a few more minutes of reading? Then we are off to the Louvre."

"Deal." Alex picked up the diary and resumed reading.

July 22nd, 1917

"*Today, we trained with the rest of the squads that make up our platoon. Keeping all the squads together and maneuvering as a section is a work of art. The one thing the French have taught me is to work as a team and be aware of what is going on to your left, right, behind, and in front of you. Always know where the NCO is; they will be your guide. In the absence of an NCO, let your training kick in. Shoot, move, communicate.*

We practiced moving by bounding or basically covering another soldier while they moved toward the enemy. It was sort of fun. I would yell, you move, and I will cover. One of my fellow soldiers would get up, run for a few seconds, get down, and yell or give the hand signal. Hand signals will be the only way to communicate when the machine guns are firing and the shells are landing when all hell opens up. You move, I will cover, and so on, till we get to where we want to go. By the way, you never run in a straight line; you always zig and zag. When we got done, I was exhausted; that was a lot of running and getting up and down. My legs are so sore."

July 25th, 1917

"*Last night was intense. It was our first time training as a unit at night. They taught us what the different color flares mean and what actions to take when you see one. First, we all lay on the ground in the prone position. It was a mostly overcast night and pitch black, with no stars visible, and a waning crescent moon. Then, all of a sudden, I heard a pop, pop, pop, and as soon as they exploded, the sky lit up. It was like daylight under the flares. I, along with everyone else, looked up at it—big mistake. Our night vision was gone. Then I heard the whistle to move out. Even with our night vision gone, it didn't matter. We could see the entire battlefield until the flares burned out. After that, it was chaos. We were stumbling over one another. After the exercise, we reassembled, and our instructor said, 'Don't look at the damn flares, do you understand. You see what happens when you do. Now, back to your positions. We will do it again till you get it right.' Needless to say, was it a late night, or was it an early morning? We will use some practice trenches in the next few days. This phase will be almost over once we have practiced working with the company and battalion.*

Based on what our French chasseurs have said, 'The trenches are their own little hell on earth.'"

"Hey, Dad, what are chasseurs?"

"Son, from what I remember, they were a light infantry unit of the French army. What set them apart was their marksmanship and the tactics they used to maneuver at high speed. Sort of like the 10th Mountain, 101st Airborne, or 82nd Airborne."

Alex nodded and continued to read. As he read the diary, people would walk by and stare at them. An elderly gentleman walking by with a cane stopped and asked in near-perfect English what he was reading, pointing to Alex.

Alex said, "A U.S. soldier's diary from World War I."

"That was before my time, but my father fought in la Première Guerre mondiale. Or what you call World War I. I was seven when the Nazis took over Paris in 1940. Those were dark days. Well, enjoy Paris, you two."

"Oui, Monsieur. Tu as une belle ville." Alex got up and shook the gentleman's hand.

"Your French is pretty good," he replied as he started to walk off.

"Sir, hold on, please," Walter said. "Your English is pretty good. Where did you learn it?"

"After the war, in the early fifties, I worked for the U.S. Forces here in Paris, and in the sixties, I lived in Chicago for a few years for work."

With excitement, Alex asked, "So, what did your dad do in the Army?"

"He was a Poilu."

"A what?" Alex asked.

Laughing, the man said, "That's an old French word for an infantryman."

Walter moved to stand next to the elderly gentleman. "Would you happen to know where the Americans were trained in France? I believe it was fairly close to Paris?"

"Hmm, no, if I remember correctly, from what my father told me, it was close to Neufchâteau, about a three-hour drive from here. Well, I must get going, or they will come and look for me. My daughter worries too much." The man waved once and ambled away.

Alex yelled after him, "Thank you!"

Walter faced Alex. "Are you thinking what I'm thinking?"

"Road trip tomorrow?" he asked.

Walter nodded as he sat back down.

Alex sat down and said, "Dad, look at the time. We need to get to the museum. We can read some more after dinner, and you need to reserve a car."

"Sounds good." Walter stood, extended his right hand, and gave the hand signal to move out.

CHAPTER 6

PREPARING FOR TRENCH WARFARE

After dinner, they returned to their room to read a little more and prepare for their road trip to Neufchâteau. Before dinner, Walter booked a car through the hotel's concierge. They were both excited: one to see some of France outside of Paris, and the second to possibly walk in the same fields the unknown soldier walked over one hundred years ago.

"Hey," Walter said. "I don't want to read too much tonight. I think it would be cool to read while we are at the place where the words were written."

"I agree, Dad."

JULY 28TH, 1917

"You know they would pick one of the hottest days of the year to play in the dirt, and let me tell you, our cotton khaki uniforms are a tad warm since we have to have all the buttons buttoned. We marched over to where the French constructed an area to simulate the trenches we would live in until

this phase was completed. Once there, they provided the trench dimensions, including its depth and width. Now, some of the trenches will have wooden planks or intertwined branches on the mud walls to support the mud wall when the artillery starts to rain in. I'm unsure how much reinforcement it gives, but it looks better than just the mud walls. Some have a small wooden walkway above the bottom of the trench to stand on. You use this level to fire from. They are not used to move around the trenches but to stand on fire or observe what's in front of the trench. On top of the trench is a dirt berm, and on top of the berm are sandbags. The height varies, but we can see how to build the berm and stack the sandbags on top of the trench. The sandbags allow us to steady the rifles and grab onto them when we go over the top and attack. Now, even though they are called sandbags, we fill them with chalk. I'm not sure if I fear the trenches or running in the open toward the Germans.

They informed us that these phases would constitute our initial training. We would learn to build and live in trenches and use different weapons while in them. There were trenches behind trenches and barbed wire everywhere. It was like a maze. When I first saw them, I thought, "How will we get over the barbed wire?" I'm sure they are going to show us.

We called the main area of the trenches 'Washington Center.' I don't think it was named after the president, but maybe it was named after the city. Once they gave an overview of the trenches, the French instructor turned to the weapons we would be using in the trenches. We all know how to fire our new rifle, the 1917 Enfields. The Enfields allow us to put ten rounds in the magazine. I really like them better than our old 1903 Springfields.

We got our hands back on the hand grenades, but this time, they showed us rifle grenades. Firing one of them is the simplest thing you can do. It's almost as easy as throwing it, but it goes a lot farther. Now, it looks nothing like a hand grenade. It resembles a can or cylinder on a long, skinny pole. You put the long, skinny pole in the barrel of your rifle. Make sure it's all the way in, and once it's secure, you pull the trigger, and it flies out of the barrel and goes in the air. Exploding where it lands. It was my first time seeing one, and I liked it. The way the French chasseurs teach is straightforward to grasp. They are so comfortable, almost cavalier, but you can see there is something in their eyes. A seriousness that only comes from having done what they are showing you. They know what they demonstrate could save your life, so we all listen intensely.

What they demonstrated to us later was the best part of the day. They call it the bunker-buster, a very small cannon but very accurate. We plan to shoot it within the next week or so. The other weapon they demonstrated was what they called a Stokes mortar. Think of a hollow tube almost standing straight, then lowering a big bullet into the tube in a second or two. You hear a thump. There goes the big bullet, but this bullet explodes when it hits the ground. It's great when the Germans are in the open on the battlefield."

"Alex, let's call it a night. We have a long day tomorrow, so we need to get up early."

Alex closed the diary and set it on the nightstand. "I'm excited about tomorrow."

ENROUTE TO NEUFCHÂTEAU, FRANCE

Walter and Alex left the hotel at 7 a.m. to drive to Lille, where the unknown soldier had trained for combat. Once they left Paris, they took the A5 southeast to Neufchâteau. As they drove, Alex read the diary.

AUGUST 5TH, 1917

"Living in the trenches is no picnic. It rained for the first couple of days, and everything was soaked. The trenches don't drain at all, and there is a lot of standing water. In the standing water, there is stuff floating, but I have no idea what it might be. Maybe I don't want to know. But the rain didn't stop the training. We slogged through the mud, getting covered head to toe in it. Well, they taught us how to get over the barbed wire. It's pretty simple: there are two ways. One is someone lying on it, and you walk/run on top of the soldier lying there. The soldier who was the guinea pig we walked over was covered in mud. I don't see how he will get his uniform and equipment clean.

They even said that if they are dead, walk on them, they won't feel it. One of the instructors even chuckled when the other said it. But not a funny chuckle like hearing a good joke, more of a nervous tic. The second is for the engineers to cut a pathway through the wire. Once you are through, they will seal the pathway so the Germans can't come through it."

AUGUST 7TH, 1917

"Yesterday was all about gas attacks. We spent the entire day. I mean the day and night. We were up twenty-four hours. In the confines of the trenches, we had to put on our gas masks and practice putting them on and defending the line. To make it as realistic as possible, a big cloud of smoke was generated and came over the battlefield in our direction. As the smoke cloud got closer, the alarms sounded. About halfway through the drill, the wind shifted and redirected the cloud back in the direction it had originated. Gas attacks can be tricky. Wind can be your friend or your worst enemy. To demonstrate the effects of the gas, the instructors brought two soldiers who had been gassed. One had scars all over his body from the mustard gas. The other could hardly be heard. His vocal cords had been damaged by chlorine. They told us about Phosgene, the deadliest gas. What makes it so lethal is that it's colorless, and you won't know you get a fatal dose till it's too late. They said it's phosgene if you smell moldy hay, especially if there's no hay around. Stop breathing and put on your mask.

I asked, 'What is the first aid for a soldier exposed to the gas?' He replied, 'It depends on the gas, but you want to get the soldier to the medical staff for treatment. Until then, keep them warm and calm if possible.'

I think the thing I fear the most is not the artillery or machine gun fire but gas."

AUGUST 10TH, 1917

"Even though it stopped raining a couple of days ago, and it's been hot with sunny days, everything is still wet and muddy in the trenches. I don't think they ever get dry. You learn to raise your gear in some cutouts along the trench walls. Our chow is brought to us from the rear, just like it would

when we are in the front. It's not bad. Hell, at least it's hot. At night, it's eerie. We can hear the shelling and machine gun fire from the frontlines. Last night, you could see the sky light up from our artillery. I started to count when I saw the light until I heard the boom. It gives you a sense of how far the round traveled. What we have been taught is that one second equals one mile. My feet have sores on them from being wet all the time. I have to change my socks at least twice a day. Everyone was issued two additional pairs of socks. I can't imagine how cold my feet are going to get. I need to bring more socks and won't leave any in the rear. Tomorrow, we are going back to the barracks in the rear. The next and last phase is about to start."

AUGUST 15TH, 1917

"I had sentry duty last night. Another soldier and I walked around the perimeter of our camp. The soldier I was with is from Boston. I had a hard time understanding him. He said he joined in February 1917 to avoid going to jail. It seems he likes to fight, so the judge gave him a choice: jail or the Army. He said he grew up poor, which we had in common. About halfway through our duty, we heard a noise and investigated it. As we got closer and closer, we saw the cause of the noise. Two raccoons had gotten tangled in the barbed wire. We both started to laugh. Two raccoons scared us. There was no telling what the Germans were going to do to us. There was no way I would touch them, so he took out his knife and cut them free. They scurried off, not to be seen again. After that fiasco, we continued guard duty. As the sun began to rise, we felt relieved. It was a long night, one of many to come."

AUGUST 18TH, 1917

"I was a runner yesterday. My job was to take orders from my unit to the higher unit and bring back any orders or other information from the higher command. Thinking I would have to run or walk the entire way made me a little nervous about whether any German snipers were somewhere in our area. I didn't think so, but you never know. As I arrived at the battalion headquarters, a motorcycle with a machine gun attached to it, resembling a baby stroller, was parked in front of the signal tent. It's the first one I have

seen up close. The driver was next to it, so I spoke with him before informing the sergeant in charge that I was reporting for duty. His face was dirty, but around his eyes, he looked like a raccoon. He told me the motorcycle was from a company called Harley-Davidson. I asked him what was attached to the motorcycle, and he replied that it was called a sidecar. I told him I would love to ride on one, but I had no idea how to drive it. He said I could volunteer as a driver or gunner. Just let him know. I will have to think about that one for a bit. He said it's like riding a bicycle with a motor. That is the only difference. It's not much different. He went over how to give power to go and how to stop it. In the middle, I heard, 'Hey, soldier, are you the runner?' I stood at attention and replied, 'Yes, sir.'

The next thing out of his mouth was, 'Get your ass over here. Take this dispatch to brigade headquarters.' I took the dispatch and started getting into the motorcycle's sidecar. He yelled, 'What the hell are you doing, soldier? That's not for you.' He pointed toward the brigade headquarters and said, 'It's only a few miles. When you get there, wait for a reply and return here.' I made four trips back and forth.

Well, needless to say, I didn't get a ride on the motorcycle, but I did a lot of running."

August 22nd, 1917

"Today, we have a day off. I spent the day cleaning my uniforms and equipment. I don't know when we will be afforded the opportunity again. I'm still hearing the artillery off in the distance. While my stuff was drying, I walked over to the hospital tent. I wanted to check on a soldier in my squad who came down with a stomach virus. I think he drank some water out of the little river next to us. When I walked in, the beds were full, not of U.S. soldiers but of French and a couple of German prisoners. I suppose we give them care just as if they were one of us. Maybe the only good thing about this war is that we can be humane to one another. They posted guards, and from the looks of them, they weren't going anywhere. I found my buddy and sat down next to him. He looked like he had been through hell, but he said he was feeling better. I replied, Well, you look like death. He laughed and said, 'How funny would it be for him to die of an illness and not by a German after all

the training we have gone through?' I gave him some water, got up, and said I would check on him again if I could.

When I got back, everything was dry. It was time to pack it up and prepare for more training."

GAS STATION: TRONVILLE-EN-BARROIS, FRANCE

After a couple of hours of driving, they stopped to get snacks and fuel in Tronville-en-Barrois. As Walter filled the rental, Alex entered the gas station and picked up a Coke and pastries. Alex put the items on the counter and said, "Hello."

The attendant replied, "Hello, are you American?"

"Yes, is it obvious?"

The attendant nodded. "Well, sort of. Driving up to Belgium?"

"Nope, we're going to Neufchâteau. We're researching World War I and where the American soldiers trained."

"I wouldn't go to Neufchâteau for that. I would go just up the road to the Gondrecourt Area, which is located before Neufchâteau. When I was in school, that's where we went on a field trip to study the war." He grabbed a map and pointed to the Gondrecourt Area.

Walter entered the store, and Alex said, "Hey, Dad. I'm sorry, what's your name?"

"Andre."

Alex continued, "Andre said we should go to the Gondrecourt Area. He said he went there on a school field trip. Alex pointed to it on the map."

"Hi, Andre. Gondrecourt Area? Hmm, well, Gondrecourt Area it is."

As they drove to the Gondrecourt Area, Alex began to read again.

AUGUST 30TH, 1917

"Sorry, it has been a while since I wrote anything, but we have been busy. Hell, we even had to cut our firewood in the woods near our camp. We used it to cook our food. The training has been challenging, but it has to be. We play

cards to pass the time at night when not out training. I have only lost a couple of bucks playing poker. I think some of these guys have played before. I'm getting pretty good with my rifle. I feel very confident with it.

The weather has turned on us. What was once a beautiful summer is now wet, damp, and miserable. There is mud everywhere. I have to clean my boots every day. Sometimes, we sit together and talk about home and what we will do when we return. I tell them about you, but they don't believe I could have a girl like you. I told them I have a great personality. Well, it's almost lights out. We must get up early. We are working with the French soldiers. They provide us with excellent training and give us real-world experience. They have fought in multiple battles and have the scars to prove it. The stories they tell us about the front are scary. But do not worry. The war will end once the Germans see us on the battlefield."

AUGUST 31ST, 1917

"A soldier was killed today. This is the first one we have lost. How he died was so stupid. Hell, not even in combat. He was run over by a truck. It seemed he decided to sleep on the ground at the back of one of the supply trucks. It was dark outside, and the driver didn't see or know he was there, backing up right over him. So now, whenever a vehicle backs up, someone must guide it back. I didn't know him very well, but I prayed for him. I might start going to services this Sunday. It seems very real now."

SEPTEMBER 1ST, 1917

"I haven't written much. We have been busy, and well, I'm tired, hell, exhausted. The good thing is that so is everyone else. I had latrine duty today. It seems I forgot to button my jacket all the way. Not going to go into much detail about what latrine duty entails, but let's say it's a crap job. I won't write in my diary daily, but I will send you a letter when possible. But when I write you a letter, I get homesick and miss you even more, if that's possible. Today, I was on one of the details, taking food and ammo to the soldiers at the front in the trenches. They say you have to practice like you are going to fight. You must do things instinctively. Don't think. Do

without thinking. Your life and the life of your fellow soldier might depend on it."

September 5th, 1917

"Today, we went to the firing range again, the third day in a row. This time, everyone got to fire different weapons. The instructors said they wanted us to have the ability and knowledge to fire our weapons and all the other weapons we could find in the trenches. I shoot the Browning Machine Gun, commonly called the Browning, a machine gun that shoots a bigger bullet at a much faster rate of fire. The downside is that it's much heavier and requires a crew of three soldiers to man it. Setting up and carrying it through the mud will be challenging.

We also got to fire some captured German weapons. I like their rifle. It's called the Gewehr 98. It's easy to fire, and it's very accurate.

After the range, we marched back to our area, where we were ambushed. Well, not by the Germans, but more of a drill. They fired bullets over our heads. As we were crawling along the ground, we heard the sound of gas alarms. We were in the middle of a simulated gas attack. Lying on the ground, heart racing, and attempting to find and put on your gas mask was, to say the least, challenging. After a few minutes, we heard the all-clear sound. We removed our masks, and the next thing was simulated wounded soldiers.

As I lay on the ground, I heard footsteps. I looked up, and there was one of the French instructors yelling at me, 'The soldier next to you has a leg wound. What are you going to do?' I replied, 'I would treat his wound.'

He grabbed me by my equipment straps and yelled, 'Don't tell me, Private, do it.' I got up, ran to the soldier, and started treating him. The instructor followed me, and as I was treating him, he said, 'Move him back to the rear, and he can't walk either.' My heart was racing, and I was breathing hard. I picked up the soldier, put him over my shoulder, and ran back to where the instructor told me to go. I got to the location where a doctor was and put the soldier on the ground. I dropped to my knees, bent over, and tried to catch my breath. As I started to catch my breath, the instructor walked over and threw the wounded soldier's rifle on the ground next to me and said,

'Private, you just gave the Germans a new rifle. One that will be used to kill your fellow Americans, or worse, a Frenchman. When I said take the soldier, I meant take him and his weapon. Now get up and get back in the formation.'

That is a lesson I won't forget anytime soon."

SEPTEMBER 12TH, 1917

"We went into one of the forests nearby and trained on how to fight in them. It's much different than in the open fields. My platoon sergeant said, 'The Germans hide snipers in the tall trees or in the tree stumps. You can't see them till they've fired. By then, they've already shot someone.' His lesson was to not just look at the ground or in front of you, but look up at the trees. We learned to maneuver through the forest. Once we reached the end, we turned around and started back in the other direction. My platoon sergeant went up to the soldier next to me and said, 'Your squad leader is dead. You're in charge. What are you going to do? You are receiving fire from a machine gun nest to your left.'

I saw the look in his eyes, one of almost hopelessness, and then, suddenly, he started giving orders to the squad. He shifted our movement toward the source of the fire, and we attacked the machine gun nest, taking it out. We did a few more iterations before returning to the barn for the night. I'm glad I didn't get called upon. I know my time is coming."

SEPTEMBER 27TH, 1917

"The entire platoon gathered today to review the training we have completed over the last few days. As we were sitting, a cavalry platoon rode by. My god, those horses were beautiful. What magnificent animals! I'm not sure I could ride one of them into battle, but I would love to ride one just for something different. We have only been here a few months; I think some guys thought the war would be over by now. Hell, we haven't even got into the fight yet."

OCTOBER 12TH, 1917

"I hope you got the letter I sent. I know it was short. As I said in the letter, don't worry about writing back. Your letters make me more homesick. I hope the little one is well. I haven't told anyone about him. I don't want any preferential treatment because I have a family. The weather is turning. There is a nip in the air, and winter is coming fast. It's starting to get cold. Sleeping in the barn is better than sleeping outside, but it's getting to everyone. There have been a few fights, but I have managed to stay out of them so far. We are all itching to get our feet wet at the front and take on the Germans. You can only train for so long. There is only so much training that can be done. The only good thing is that we can visit the local village, stop in the café, and have a glass of red wine. They call it vin rouge. It's damn good. Lately, we have the ongoing sound of artillery in the background: boom, boom. The sound is complex to describe; it is very deep-throated. I don't know if it's our artillery training or if the Germans are that close. I sleep with my rifle. Kinda getting used to the sounds of the artillery and can sleep through most of it. The day is getting nearer, and we will be on the receiving end of the German guns. They say you never hear the one that gets you. I want to hear every one of them.

One thing they continue to drill into our heads is the brutality of the enemy. They must be killed, severely disabled, or captured. They can, under no circumstances, be left to their own free will, no matter how fast we are advancing. You kill them, or they will kill you. It's war! It was a common theme every day, hammered in our heads.

To emphasize the point, we practiced bayonet and hand-to-hand combat training, and learned how to kill quickly by piercing the heart area if possible. Whether the bayonet is in our hands or attached to our rifles. To practice the bayonet on the rifle, they had set up a course where we would run toward a wooden structure where four life-size burlap sacks filled with hay were hung. They called them dummies. On the dummies were painted red circles, indicating where to thrust your bayonet, causing the most severe and life-threatening wounds to the human body. I ran up to the sack, took the rifle, and with the butt, came around and hit the dummy in the head. I then pulled back the rifle and thrust the bayonet into its chest, pulled it out, and thrust it into another section of the dummy, yelling the entire time.

After completing the rifle bayonet training, we moved on to practicing and honing our skills in killing with only the bayonet. We took off the bayonet and practiced on one another. I took my bayonet in my right hand and came up behind the other soldier, grabbed his head, and put the blade across his neck. Once I slit his throat, I stabbed him in the kidney area. After everyone had completed a few practice drills, we returned to the hay dummies and continued for the next couple of hours. Once we finished with the bayonet, we took out our trench knife and used it to drill. It's a little shorter than the bayonet but just as deadly. That is one way I would hate to die, getting stabbed or my throat cut while fighting in a trench."

CHAPTER 7

THE FIRST CASUALTIES

GONDRECOURT TRAINING AREA, FRANCE

Walter and Alex walked around Gondrecourt and the Rolampont training area. After wandering around the area, they stopped at a local café and bought a couple of coffees and pastries. As they sat in the café, Alex took out the diary and read from it, then stopped. "It's strange, but I feel connected to the soldier. I can't explain it."

"I guess that could happen," Walter said. "Or maybe it's because of the emotions he put in the diary. It's powerful, to say the least, and we haven't even gotten to him being in combat."

OCTOBER 22ND, 1917

"It is all too real now, no longer an imaginary enemy. They are in front of us. Yesterday, we were brought up to the front and are currently manning the trenches alongside our French allies. Where we are, the landscape, I imagine, was once beautiful, with its rolling hills covered in trees and tall grass, next to a flowing river. It is now a barren piece of land pockmarked by artillery shelling. At different times, I could see families having picnics and rowing down the river in a wooden rowboat. But that was not to be. I have

never studied war, but this is a perfect place for war. It's open, and the fields of fire are great. I could hear the cannons firing. They were very loud, and we were a lot closer to them. I can also hear machine guns and rifles firing theirs and ours. The one thing I can't hear is the screams from the soldiers, for now.

Even with the enemy close, we are excited to finally move up to the front. This is another phase of our training, so we are somewhat shielded. There is a sense of pride today, just like when we landed in France all those months ago. There is a renewed pep in our step. Our shoulders are back, and our chests are out—like toy soldiers."

OCTOBER 23RD, 1917

"Yesterday was pretty exciting after I added my notes to my diary, and as I was putting it away. I heard the sound of artillery, not the Germans or French, but ours. We are in the fight. Our artillery fired their first rounds yesterday. We continue to practice with our gas masks. We had a false alarm yesterday. We heard the sounds of sirens signaling a gas attack, but it was just smoke shells. They were used to conceal a German patrol as it tried to enter our perimeter. The M1917 Browning machine gun next to my position along the trench opened up on them. They didn't stand a chance. When I looked up after, the machine gun went silent. German soldiers lay on the ground, hanging on the wire and walking back to their lines as they bled out. They would never make it. I could hear the moans of the wounded. That is a sound I won't forget."

OCTOBER 25 - 29TH, 1917

"I heard there were some wounded soldiers, but they were treated in the French field hospital. I didn't hear the severity of their wounds, but I prayed for them. I'm not sure what happened or what unit they were assigned to. They won't be the last we will have. I need to practice my first-aid skills.

The news spread that our unit had captured its first German prisoner. A joint French and American patrol captured him as he wandered off to use the latrine. They caught him with his pants down. I guess they sent him back to the rear for interrogation. *I wonder if they let him finish. I didn't get to see him, but the story of his capture spread like wildfire through our camp.*

On a different topic, we got some of our winter gear. One piece of gear is a long wool coat, which they call a trench coat. Where do you think they got the name? Comes from the British. It's damn warm, and I can stay warm even if wet. Based on the weather so far, I will get a lot of use out of it.

October 31st, 1917

"Yesterday, a soldier approached me and said, 'You are always writing in that book. I don't write so well. Can you write a letter for me to my ma and pa?' I guess I'm a sucker, but I felt compelled to write the letter. I couldn't help but ask if anyone back home could read. He replied that his younger sister could read really well.

I said, 'Well, let's get to it.' As he told me what to write, I could imagine his family back home sitting on the porch, reading his letter out loud.

Last night was quiet. There was a full moon and clear skies, and I could see the entire battlefield from where I was in the trench, manning the bunker-buster, the 37mm M1916. I didn't get to shoot it, but I was ready. The trenches are muddy, as can be, and it's getting cold at night. I can see the water freeze when it gets really cold. It seems like almost everyone has a cold. Every once in a while, I can hear a single rifle shot, a sniper. Nobody was hit. I guess the Germans must have been bored.

Today is Halloween. There's not a lot of trick-or-treating, but we have a lot of candy. I have quite a sweet tooth. I really like the Peanut Chews and the Clark Bar."

November 4th, 1917

"Every night until last was quiet other than an occasional rifle shot. Last night was different. German artillery opened fire at around 3:00 a.m. A unit to our right was taking the brunt of the fire. Suddenly, flares and alarms sounded along the front. When the shells impacted the ground, dirt flew up along with the pieces of metal, some large and most very small, piercing everything they hit. We heard the screams of our fellow soldiers

taking fire as we continued to man our positions, not sure what the Germans were up to. Once the artillery stopped, my platoon was ordered to the position of the wounded soldiers. When we got there, the German raiders had left their mark. They used Bangalore torpedoes to cut a path through the barbed wire and move undetected to the trenches. I decided to put tin cans in our wire in front of our trenches. Maybe we could hear them before breaching our defenses. As the raiders moved into the trenches, pistols emerged, and bayonets were fixed to their Mausers. The soldiers in the trenches didn't stand a chance. The attack caught everyone by surprise. Some of the bodies lay waste from hand grenades. What a lethal weapon. Anything within a fifteen-foot radius would be killed or severely wounded. As we moved along the trench, there were soldiers with their throats cut lying in the water. Some face up, and some face down. Not one German had been killed. But kill they did, the ones they didn't, they took as prisoners.

As I helped get my comrades, I couldn't help but notice all of them lying in the bloody, muddy trench. The water was high enough in a section of the trench that the bodies were floating. I walked into another section of the trench, and the skeletons of soldiers lay there. They looked like German soldiers from battles long ago, based on their uniforms. Our French instructors were right. The trenches are their own little hell on earth. For us, this was the first time in this war that U.S. soldiers laid down their lives for their country on foreign soil. God rest their souls.

No one slept the rest of the night."

NOVEMBER 6TH, 1917

"The other day, we went on our first patrol with the French. The lessons they have taught us are lifesaving. We made our way to a dried-out creek bed and crawled to where it went into a bombed-out village. We exited from the creek bed and formed two columns to move through the village. As we moved, we were taught how to clear a house and cover each other in an urban area. About halfway through the village, one of the guys in my squad took a round in the arm, and our French instructor was right on him. He moved him behind a short wall and began providing first aid. At the same time, he

instructed us on what to do in the event of an injury. The bullet grazed his arm. A nice bandage, and he was good to go.

While he was treating him, we got into a defensive position to shield them. I saw where the bullet that hit him came from—and noticed the flash from the barrel. Hell, I hope he was not shooting at me. I brought my rifle up, aimed it, and fired two rounds. I wasn't nervous at all. The rifle held steady in my hands. I took a deep breath, let it out, took another, and held it. I put my trigger finger on the trigger and gently pulled it, not moving the rifle at all. The rifle recoiled in my shoulder, but I kept the aim and was ready to fire another shot. Now, I'm not sure if I hit him, but there was no more shooting from that window.

All the training we have been doing for the last few months is paying off. After treating the wounded soldier, the French soldier took two men to where the sniper was located to see if he had been hit. My squad leader came and patted me on the back and said, 'Good reaction, Soldier.'

The patrol came back, and the French soldier said, 'Nice kill.' The sniper was the first person I have ever killed ..."

November 8th, 1917

"We held a small but dignified ceremony for our fallen comrades. The bodies were brought from the trenches where they died in the German raid the other night. My platoon was assigned to escort the bodies to the rear so they could have their last rites read to them. After that, they were laid to rest in Bathelemont, a town ravaged by years of war. Both the American and French armies paid their respects. I looked at the faces of my fellow soldiers. A little of the glamor of war was out of their eyes. We all knew this would not be the last time we laid to rest our fellow countrymen, or maybe one day. They would be paying their respects to one of us. Once their bodies were laid to rest, a twenty-one-gun salute was heard, three volleys from seven rifles. After the twenty-one-gun salute, the solemn sound of a bugle playing taps could be heard in the distance. Something about taps brings tears to my eyes every time I listen to it. I know I will shed many tears in this war. Perhaps one day, there will be no tears left for me to shed. There will be no more I can shed."

Alex closed the diary and glanced over at his dad. "What are taps?"

"Taps are played to honor the fallen military members and are done at the end of the ceremony."

"Will you have taps played at your funeral?"

His father nodded solemnly. "Yes, just like your grandfather."

"Come on, let's get something to eat."

As they got up, Alex hugged his dad, and he hugged him back. Walter didn't want to let go, so he said softly to his son, "This is what I needed. It's a good day."

"Yes, Dad, it's one of many to come."

NOVEMBER 20TH, 1917

"Now that our rotation at the front is over, a lot is going on. We were relieved and marched back to the rear last night. As we marched down the road, I had never seen so many pieces of artillery and machine guns. Trucks lined the road, causing traffic jams. I looked up, waiting for a German airplane to dive and strafe us. I don't think they fly much at night, or at least I hope so. As we continued to move to the rear, it appeared that the entire division was concentrated in one place.

As we marched by, I noticed that some of the soldiers looked like they had just arrived from the transport ships from the States. They were the replacements for the soldiers killed. By the number of them, the generals were planning for a lot of dead soldiers. The look on their faces versus ours was striking. Yet, I remembered that look. It was the same one we had many months ago.

This is our final phase of training. The next time we move to the front, it won't be training. It will be for life or death."

DECEMBER 6TH, 1917

"Yesterday was crazy. We were not in the trenches but in front of them doing what they call 'Open Warfare.' In what once was, I assume, a beautiful field or thin forest. Now, it's just a pockmarked piece of dirt and mud with tree stumps no more than five feet tall. The field smelled of contaminated

water, and something I couldn't determine was a strange new smell. The fields we were in had been fought over for the last three years. Many soldiers from both sides had died on them. That scent, I know I will smell till I get out of here. Nothing is living or growing- well, maybe the rats.

Our day started at daybreak with an artillery barrage on the simulated enemy target. The noise was deafening when the shells impacted. As the shells were flying in and starting to impact, we were given the signal to advance. One platoon would move, then another, and even though no one was shooting at us, we kept low while we ran. Once we reached our position, the other platoon would move, and we would cover them. I was out of breath. We are carrying all our equipment and extra ammo. They even gave us ammo for the machine guns. While we were moving the machine guns, they would move into place and begin firing. I can't describe how many bullets they can fire in a minute. The only way I may be able to explain it is by clicking your middle finger and thumb together as fast as you can, and that is not even how quickly they fire. They fire so rapidly that the ammunition is loaded onto a belt and fed into the machine gun. I'm glad we have them, but so do the Germans, who are very effective with them. I have seen it first-hand.

Once we got to the objective, the platoon leader reviewed what we did right and what we didn't. As the day went on, we did more right than wrong. I heard a rumor that we have a few more days of this. One good thing is that after the day's activities, we would march back to the barracks with a hot meal waiting for us. I could get used to this, but I'd better not. Christmas is right around the corner, our first one apart."

December 10th, 1917

"I can't believe how cold it gets here. Everything has frost on it. Everyone is looking forward to Christmas. We are planning something special for the local townspeople. It's the least we can do. We have taken over their towns and farms.

The ground we are drilling on is frozen solid. When you hit the ground on your belly, it's like diving on concrete; we tried digging foxholes, but that didn't go too well. I have no idea how we are going to bury our dead in the frozen ground."

DECEMBER 25TH, 1917

"Kindness can be found even in the worst conditions known to man; you don't have to look far. The compassion that lies in a man's heart is, at times, overwhelming, and those same hearts are trained to kill their fellow man. But today, our hearts are with the French citizens. We decided to give back to the French children. These children may only know war and killing, so we wanted to bring some happiness and joy and give them a little time of peace and hope. So, we decorated for Christmas. A few men went into Paris, and they must have cleaned out the stores of everything from decorations to candy and gifts.

A couple of men from each barracks went into the forest, cut down a tree for each barracks, and decorated it for Christmas. Once we were done, the citizens of this great town came through each barracks, and the children got candy and a small gift. However, their parents got the best gift. The gift of seeing their children being children. The joy in their eyes, the laughter, and the shouts of joy when they received a present and candy make what we are doing here worthwhile. Everyone misses their families, but today, this town is our family. Merry Christmas, 1917."

JANUARY 3RD, 1918

"It's a new year. We had a nice New Year's Eve celebration. It will be the last one for a while. Our training is done or will be in a couple of days, and we will be on our way to the front. We are ready! The American and French officers and NCOs have done a great job preparing us for what lies ahead. The soldier I wrote the letter to a while ago asked me to write another. He was telling me all about where he was from—a little town in Central Arkansas, Bald Knob. He said his family was farmers, with strawberry and cotton fields as far as the eye could see. He and his siblings would go out in the fields and pick strawberries all day. Laughing, he said he ate more than he brought home. He could always tell when his little brother ate the strawberries. He would look like he had red lipstick on. I could see in his eyes that he was missing helping his family make a living. As he talked, I sometimes closed my eyes and saw myself in a strawberry patch, leaning down in the hot

sun and picking and eating some of them. I realized how much I miss fresh fruit.

His father came from County Cork, Ireland, and settled there a few years ago. After going through Ellis Island, his father settled in upstate New York with his older brother. However, after a few months, he decided to move to Mississippi. There, he met his wife. From there, they moved to Arkansas to farm. They didn't own the farm, but they worked it for free in a house next to the fields.

He is the oldest son of eleven kids, and somehow, he remembers each of their names. He is a nice guy. I'm going to keep my eyes on him. He quit school and can't read well; his writing is even worse. I should tutor him so he can write his own letters home one day. Maybe something good can come out of this war.

I packed up all my gear. We are moving out in the next couple of days."

CHAPTER 8

TO THE FRONT

PLACE DES CORDELIERS: NEUFCHÂTEAU, FRANCE

Walter and Alex stood next to the tall concrete monument, a memorial for the 149 men who fell from Neufchâteau in World War I. The monument was updated after World War II to add the names of those residents who fell in that war. Neufchâteau had seen its share of war and death.

When they were done admiring the beautiful sculpture, Alex said, "Let's sit over there and read more. It's such a lovely day."

VICINITY OF FRONT LINES: BOUCONVILLE, FRANCE

JANUARY 5TH, 1918

"It started to snow last night and has not stopped. The ground looks so beautiful, covered in snow. But we all know what lies under the snow. We got our orders to move out yesterday. It's going to be a long, cold march. Maybe we will get a ride on one of the trucks going to the front. Wishful thinking, as much as we have been marching lately, our bodies can take what they dish out."

JANUARY 18TH, 1918

"The march up here was long and hard. We all got issued some new equipment, which added to the weight of what we were already carrying. I think all the gear weighs fifty-five pounds. Here is a list of the contents of our packs:

2 – Wool Blankets
Extra Rations
One side of a tent
Extra shoes
Mess Kit
Underwear
Entrenching Tool (E-Tool)

All that was in our packs; we still had to carry our steel helmets, rifles, extra ammunition, bayonets, trench knives, and gas masks. The weather was tolerable, but then it started to rain on the 2nd day, and then it sleeted. I was miserable. Everything I had on was drenched. Once we stopped to eat our cold sandwiches, I was shivering. I couldn't wait to get going again. I hoped that everything in my pack wasn't soaked. But I didn't find out till we reached our destination. I needed to wear some dry clothes or at least put on a pair of dry socks. Once we started on the march, the road was again snowy and icy. It gets freezing cold in France.

When we reached our initial area, I opened my pack and took out some clothes. I was happy that most of my clothes were dry. I must have packed them right. I had a dry pair of socks, pants, and a shirt. My long coat will take some time to dry, but at least it's made of wool and keeps me warm, even when it's wet. But damn, it gets heavy when it's wet."

JANUARY 24TH, 1918

"As we marched up to the front, civilians from the towns and villages near the front walked past us on their way from the fighting and front lines. The column of civilians went for miles, most of them walking, some of the young and elderly on carts with their worldly possessions. Most of them didn't have warm clothes. They all looked malnourished. I handed my rations to the mother and her child. The little girl held what was left of her baby doll

as if her life depended on it. Maybe it did. But the looks on their faces said it all. The years of war had taken a toll on every one of them. The effects of war aren't just reserved for soldiers. Not one of them had their head down. Despite all the pain and suffering, they remain a proud nation. My resolve to fight for them is stronger than ever.

Our unit replaced one of the French units the other day. We are on the front and have taken our positions. I'm next to a machine gun team. So far, they haven't had to fire it. I would have thought the Germans would have attacked when we did the changeover from the French to us. My back has been killing me since the march, but my feet are dry now. I hung my wet socks on a rope line tied from one side of the trench to the other to dry. I'm glad we haven't had to march anywhere yet. It gives my socks a chance to dry. My platoon sergeant came to my position and pointed to a hill in the near distance. He told me the Germans owned the highest point in the area and sometimes would put a shot off or two in our direction. He told me to pass it along the trench line so all the soldiers would be informed and keep their heads down. When he left, I put my head down a little lower. I don't want to become a statistic.

By the end of the day, we had to dig out the trenches. We are all standing in inches of mud. My once-dry feet are now soaked and damn cold. When your feet are wet and you don't change your socks, you get what they call 'trench foot.' The skin on your feet will fall off, and it takes a long time to heal. From what I've been told, it causes a lot of pain and is difficult to get rid of in this damp climate. I don't want to get trench foot or frostbite. The trenches are not draining at all, which keeps our feet wet. They are not as deep as the ones we trained in. Maybe the French soldiers were shorter than we. So, when we have time, we dig and dig."

JANUARY 26TH, 1918

"I was assigned to a team to go out of the trench and create wire obstacles. As we put out the wire, we came under an artillery attack. Thank God they were off, and only a couple of soldiers got wounded by the shrapnel from the blast. The sky was alight from the shells when they impacted. Once the shells started coming in, I hit the ground and put my hands on my helmet. The sounds were deafening, louder than before. Maybe it's another type of cannon. The barrage lasted a couple of minutes. As the Germans were firing, I could hear our artillery start to fire. As our rounds went over my head whistling, I put up my fist and yelled, 'Take that, you Huns.' That's a name I heard the Germans being called. Our rounds must have gotten close because the Germans stopped firing. I waited for the machine gun fire to stop, but it continued for a few more minutes. The battlefield was eerily silent during the lull in the shelling and machine gun fire. I noticed something during the silence. There was only one sound, not the birds or farm animals. It was the rats. It would have been completely quiet and spooky if it weren't for them. However, despite the artillery attack and the harassment from the machine guns, we successfully completed our mission. As I lay there, not hearing anything, I remembered what our commander had said as we moved into position: 'This is a quiet area, not much activity.' I wonder if I should tell him someone didn't tell him the truth. That barrage and machine gun fire was not what I would consider quiet.

I'm pretty proud! We completed our mission, and the wire obstacles are in place. As I got up to move back to the trench, I looked over and saw more trenches in front of us. I have a feeling that I will see the inside of them very shortly. It seems this war is about inches and feet. Like a tug-of-war for land, the soldiers fighting are being pulled back and forth over trenches.

FEBRUARY 4TH, 1918

"Today was a good day, but bitterly cold. I got some sleep and dried my socks over a small fire while we made some coffee. I can't tell you how great they felt when I put them on. I'm starting to wear my other pair of boots, and even though they aren't waterproof or insulated, they feel comfortable. However, I still need to break them in.

I had to pull guard duty at the dugout the company commander used as his company headquarters. It wasn't bad; a few hours were on duty and a few off. The company commander came by and asked me how I was doing. I told him I was doing great. He smiled and walked into the dugout. He seemed like a nice man. I haven't had any interaction with him, nor do I want any. Typically, when you talk to him, you're in trouble or get a medal. I don't need any medals and try to stay out of trouble. All I need is you.

I can guess that by the amount of activity, something is up. I cleaned my rifle and checked all my gear when I got off. I even practiced putting on my gas mask. I told the guys they should do the same. One of the other soldiers said, 'I worried too much about the gas attacks.' When I was done, I found a couple of pieces of wood. I put them down and sat on them. I had enough room for one of the other young soldiers to sit beside me. He seemed very nervous, or I think anxious is a better word. He was watching me write in my diary. He told me he lost his diary a few weeks ago, but it didn't matter. He never wrote in it. I asked him if he was okay, and he replied that he was fine. I don't believe him. His hands were shaking, and not from the cold. I looked at him and continued writing."

"Dad, who do you think this soldier is?"

"That's a good question. I don't know, but his writings suggest he is educated. I would say rather young, even though the average age of a U.S. soldier in World War I was twenty-six, maybe early twenties, and he's an infantryman."

"Do you think he's married?" Alex asked.

"I do. Based on when he wrote about not wanting anyone to know he has a son. He may be from the East Coast or the Midwest, and he volunteered for the Army. The draft didn't start until May 18th, 1917."

"Why's that?"

"He was on the first transports to France. They left in June 1917, and he was already established in his unit by then. Are you ready to go?"

"Just a few more pages, and yep, I'm getting hungry. I saw a great place around the corner."

His father nodded for him to continue reading.

FEBRUARY 10TH, 1918

"I went out on patrol last night. I'm getting good at working in the dark. I can't say how or where we went over the wire. Even though it was my first night patrol, I was not scared, just nervous. The squad I was with had already completed a couple, and they were short a man, so I was assigned to them for the mission. As we started to move through what is called 'No man's land,' the Germans popped a flare. We froze in our tracks and got down on the ground. I'm not sure if they saw or heard us, but a machine gun opened up, and the sky was ablaze with white and green tracer rounds coming at us from all directions. The bullets from the machine gun impacted in front of me, and dirt was flying up in the air and hitting me in the face. I could feel the grains of dirt hit my helmet. I'm so glad we have these new helmets. The flare fell to the ground, and it was pitch dark again. The machine gun fire stopped. We got up and started our movement toward the Germans.

Suddenly, the night sky was lit up again by German flares. It was like daylight. I got as low to the frozen ground as possible. I pulled out my bayonet and attached it to my rifle. The squad leader shot a flare to expose where we were receiving fire. While the flare descended to the ground, I looked out into 'No man's land' and saw them behind a berm. They were only one hundred yards away and straight in front of us. They had a clear field of fire. The only thing between them and us was a couple of tree stumps. My heart was pumping like never before. I could feel it in my temples. All of a sudden, I heard the sound of metal on metal. I looked over to the soldier on my right. He just lay there. Half his head was gone. He took a round in the head, and it went right through his helmet. He didn't make a sound. He died in an instant. What I ate for dinner came up. I have never seen a wound like that. The machine gun was still firing when I heard the whistle to advance. We had to take the machine gun emplacement out of action. I crawled over to the soldier, put my hand in his shirt, and felt around for his identification tags. I grabbed his identification tags, pulled one off, and left the other with the body so he could be identified.

The squad leader motioned for me to move forward. I got up, and my legs felt like Jell-O, but I ran like I had never run in my entire life. He covered my movement as I zigged and zagged in the open field. The enemy's rounds impacted all around me and whizzed by my head, but none hit me. I was hoping they wouldn't be able to lock on to me or, if they did, kill me quickly. I ran for about ten yards and dropped to the ground. I motioned the squad leader to move forward as I covered him. As the squad was moving, another soldier fell, this time to my left. I heard him screaming, but there was nothing I could do. I tried to shut his screams out, but I couldn't. I had to move forward, and as I did, he continued to scream. It was a scream unlike any I have ever heard, unlike hitting your thumb with a hammer—a primitive or primal scream.

I looked up and saw that I was only twenty yards from the machine gun. All of a sudden, I hear a boom, boom. Two hand grenades were thrown in the emplacement. The sound of machine gun fire was gone. I ran up to the emplacement with my bayonet fixed. I was going to stab a German. There was so much rage in my heart. One of my fellow soldiers was dead. The other, well, I didn't know if he was dead or alive.

As I jumped into the machine gun emplacement, three German soldiers wore field-gray uniforms, wool overcoats, and Stahlhelm helmets painted in camouflage. They lay in body parts, some large, some small. Legs and arms contorted in unnatural positions. I could tell which soldier took the brunt of the explosion. The hand grenade did its job. There wasn't much for me to stab. I raised my rifle, held it there, and then lowered it. I couldn't do it. The rage was gone. I dropped to my knees and prayed. As I was praying, the squad leader told me to search the bodies. It was like a rite of passage.

I went to the first soldier, or what was left of him, and combed through his pockets. He had a lighter and some cigarettes. I found his army papers and took them. The next soldier was the sergeant. He had a submachine gun, two stick grenades, a map, a lighter, cigarettes, and a letter from his wife or girlfriend. I took his papers and put them with the other. The third soldier only had his papers. He looked very young, maybe eighteen. I opened his papers, but I have no idea what they said; I don't read German. I picked up all the documents and handed them to the squad leader.

Along with the German papers, I gave the dead soldier's ID tag to the squad leader. He looked at me and said, 'Thank you. He was a friend of mine.' I put my hand on his shoulder and replied, 'He didn't feel anything. He was never in pain.' He nodded and put the ID tag in his right pocket—the papers from the Germans he put in his pouch. I picked up their rifles and other weapons, and I went over to where the machine gun was positioned. It was an MG08/15. There was still a belt of ammo hanging out of it. They looked like they were in for a fight based on how much ammo they had. The other thing I noticed was that there was no food or water; they hadn't been there long, or they were going to get resupplied. The question was when they were going to get resupplied.

After taking the machine gun out, another infantry platoon came up on our rear from the trenches. Once they were in position, we were ordered back to the trenches. As we moved back, I could see a stretcher-bearer working on the wounded soldier. I looked over and lifted my head as if asking a question. He glanced at me and shrugged. His screaming had stopped. I didn't know if it was from something the stretcher-bearer gave him or if he was dead."

Alex closed the diary and looked at his dad. "I think I'm done for the day."

"Yeah, war isn't like the movies."

Alex put his head back and closed his eyes. With his eyes closed, he could see the battle play out in his mind.

He opened his eyes and said, "Dad, let's return to Paris. We can walk around and enjoy the lights of the city."

ENROUTE: PARIS, FRANCE

As Walter drove back to Paris, Alex leaned back and slept. While sleeping, he dreamed of what he had just read. He could see the entire scene play out in his head. What he couldn't see was the face of the unknown soldier who wrote the diary. He could see the faces of his fellow soldiers and those of the Germans, or what was left of the faces.

"Hey, Alex, wake up. You're having a nightmare." His dad grabbed his arm.

"What, is everything okay?" Alex asked.

"Yes, you were having a nightmare. You kept saying, 'I'm going to stab him.' Over and over."

"Wow, Dad, I could see this diary in my dreams. It played out in my mind."

"Well, maybe we should put that away for a while."

"No, I'm good. Dad, his face is the only one I couldn't see. How much longer to Paris?"

"Thirty minutes or so. Perfect timing."

CHAPTER 9

RAIDING PARTY

Alex got up early after a restful night, after the dream he had had driving back from Neufchâteau. His dad woke shortly after him and sat in bed when Alex took out the diary and started reading. "Son, you are up early. Did you sleep okay?"

"Oh, yes, slept like a baby." Are you ready to start today's activities? Dad, we only have a few more days in France."

"Damn, you're right. What would you like to do today?" Walter asked.

"How about we visit Versailles?"

"How about we do that the day before we leave? Let me surprise you. We can either take the car or the train. You choose."

"I'm a car guy, Dad. We can just hop in the car if we want to go somewhere else."

"Like father, like son," Walter replied.

"Yep, as it should be! I'm going to read a little. You need to get ready, Soldier," Alex said, smiling.

FEBRUARY 15TH, 1918

"Today was a down day for the platoon, mostly cleaning our equipment and getting some rest. After the last couple of days, it was nice to try to relax. I played some cards with the guys and had a good time, enjoying some laughs along the way. I think we all need to laugh a little. I can see a difference in how some of the fellows act. They are very cautious and more deliberate. Everyone is still upbeat. We feel good about what we are doing here. We know we are going to lose friends in the war, but we can't let the Germans control Europe.

When we get new soldiers, some of the soldiers in the platoon don't even try to learn their names. Heck, almost everyone has a nickname; even the trenches have nicknames. We even named our trench 'Jersey.' Slugger gave the trench its name. He is from New Jersey, the state, and it stuck. Why do I call him Slugger? He played baseball before joining the Army. Where some of the trenches come together is called 'Times Square.' Give soldiers a little free time, and we can come up with some crazy things."

FEBRUARY 20TH, 1918

"The French unit that was here before we took over is training us for raiding parties. No, it's not like parties at home. These are for capturing prisoners and gathering intelligence. I'm pretty excited to be part of the raiders. The French team is a Moroccan raiding specialist that has been conducting raids for some time. All the training has been at night. The other night was our first training session, and all I could think about was my first night patrol and seeing the soldier next to me with half his head gone. I have to stop thinking about it and focus, or that is going to be me. They showed us how to infiltrate the German defenses and the layout of their trenches. We even practiced hand-to-hand combat in the trenches. Hand-to-hand combat in the trenches has to be the most animalistic way to kill someone. There is very little room to maneuver. The first one to get his jab is almost always the winner, the one who lives to see another day.

After the training, I sat down with one of the Moroccan soldiers. He was a very soft-spoken older man. He told me about his country. It's someplace I would like to visit. He lives on the coast near the Mediterranean Sea in northern Africa. His family has been living in the same house for hundreds of years. Before the war, he was a sheep herder. His herd consisted of hundreds of sheep when he left for the war. When he talked about home, he spoke of someplace he had been but would never return to. It's almost like he was resigned to die here in France. I hope I never talk like that. Once happy and carefree, war changes men who looked to the future but now talk about the past, who are living minute by minute."

February 22nd, 1918

"Two nights of raids, and we captured over twenty Germans—even a couple of high-ranking officers. There were two different targets for the raids. The one I was assigned went over the wire after our engineers blew holes in the German wire. We made our way into a German trench that looked like it had been abandoned the day before, from a relentless artillery barrage from our guns. I don't see how anyone could have survived. We watched it from our trenches; the sky lit like the 4th of July.

When I jumped into the trench, I landed on a German soldier. As I got to my feet, his face was right before me. His eyes were wide open. It was as if he were staring at me, looking into my soul. I jumped back and bayoneted him. I didn't know if he was dead or alive. I know he is dead now. The squad started moving through the trench. I could have sworn the French soldier knew his way around the trench like he was the one who had built it. Hell, maybe he did. After a few minutes, we stopped and waited for an artillery barrage to commence. It seemed like I sat there for hours, but it was only thirty minutes. Then, all of a sudden, I could see the impact from the shells, and the ground started to vibrate and violently shake. The water at the bottom of the trench rippled as if something were under it. Then, pieces of dirt fell from the walls. It might cave in on us, but we didn't move. That was the closest I have ever been to the receiving end of an artillery barrage.

As the barrage moved further north, we began to move. We wanted to be at our other target, but there was some confusion, and we thought more shells would rain on them. As we turned a corner, four German soldiers came running toward us. They didn't even notice we weren't Germans till it was too late. My squad leader tripped the first one, and the other fell over him. I grabbed the one on top and pushed him face-first against the trench wall. My right arm was on his neck, and my left hand gripped my bayonet. I kicked him in the back of his knee, and he dropped. He was saying something in German, but I didn't understand. The rest of the squad had the other three Germans under control. With my bayonet touching his ribs, one of the other soldiers tied his hands behind his back. As I was pulling him up by the rope, one of the other Germans started running back toward the way he came from, yelling, 'Americans, Americans.' He only got a couple of yards before another soldier hit him in the back of his head with the butt of his rifle. He slammed to the ground like a sack of potatoes. The French soldier told us to move. His comrades might have heard him. He kicked the soldier on the ground. He didn't move, but he made a sound.

There was no way we would carry him back to our lines. The French soldier took out his knife and slit his throat. Blood squirted out of his throat on the French soldier's face. I could hear the gurgling from the dying soldier. He leaned down and searched the dying soldier. When he was finished, he turned around, and I saw his expressionless, emotionless face and cold eyes. I didn't see one emotion; I was just blank. As he walked by me, he said, 'You don't let them live.' He didn't even wipe off the dead German's blood.

We made it back with the other three. I didn't sleep well when we got back. All I could see was that expressionless face. God, I hope I make it out of here with emotions."

MARCH 1st, 1918

"On the 26th of February, the rest of my unit and I were awakened by the sound of the gas alarms. Then, the Germans unleashed a barrage of artillery with a mix of high explosives and mustard gas. My heart was beating fast. I started breathing faster and faster. I had to calm myself down, but all I could think of was where I put my gas mask. It was pitch black, and the only light came from the shells as they impacted the ground. I fumbled for a few seconds before my hands stumbled on it, right where I left it. When panic sets in, your mind will play tricks on you. Once my mask was on, my heart rate slowed, and my breathing returned to normal.

I put on my mask and moved to my position along the line, thinking surely the Germans were about to attack. I popped my head over the berm, and when a shell exploded, I could see the cloud of gas coming my way. The wind was blowing directly into the trench. It would be upon me in minutes. I rechecked my mask to ensure it was sealed. I looked to my left, and the soldier was in a state of full panic. He couldn't get his mask on. I reached over and shook him, and helped him put it on. The fear in his eyes was primal. This was the same soldier who ridiculed me for practicing putting my gas mask on.

After checking his mask, I could see the cloud of gas over my head. My mask worked, and so did the soldiers next to me. Further down the line, I heard a scream, and racing toward me was a soldier with no gas mask on. He couldn't breathe. Gasping for breath, he said in a raspy voice, 'Help me,' as he ran by me. There was nothing I could do. I looked back up, and I could see the German infantry advancing in the distance by the light of the flares.

I checked to verify my rifle was loaded, and I put extra ammo next to me in the cubby hole. All of a sudden, our artillery impacted where the Germans were. I saw soldiers flying in the air. Dirt was flying everywhere. Where there was water, it would spray like a fountain. The sky lit up almost as if it were daylight. They kept advancing toward me. I started firing and aiming as steadily as I could. My adrenaline was pumping. To my left and right, the Browning Machine Guns opened fire. I saw the tracer rounds hitting the German soldiers as they ran, one after another, falling to the ground. The cloud of gas was over the entire unit. I could hear the screams of the soldiers where the gas was doing what it intended to do. I shut them out, aimed, and fired my rifle.

Off in the distance, in the trenches to my far right, the Germans had overtaken the trench. I could hear the hand-to-hand combat. My first instinct was to run over and assist, but I couldn't leave my position. The Germans in our sector were repelled, and as they retreated, the artillery continued to rain in on them. It looked like half of them were missing from the original attacking force. The fighting continued to my right, but was coming to an end. The Germans who had entered the trench were either killed, wounded, or captured. By the grace of God, the wind shifted, the cloud of gas was gone, and we got the all-clear signal.

Even after hearing the all-clear signal, I hesitated to remove my mask.

When I did, it was like the first time I breathed fresh air. Like training, it was soaked from my sweat. I turned it inside out to let it dry. As I was doing that, I heard my squad leader moving down the trench, checking on all of us. I could tell we had dead among us. I looked to my left. The soldier I helped with his mask was one of them. He took a round in his helmet. He died quickly, not like the ones who died a painful death from gas or had the long-term effects of the poison gas, like blindness. Maybe he was the lucky one. Later that night, I realized I didn't even know his name. He was one of the new guys.

Once everything calmed down, we reloaded our magazines, cleaned our weapons, got some chow, and waited till the next attack. We were spread pretty thin after this attack. I hope we get some replacements soon. It's going to be daylight in a couple of hours. I need some rest."

MARCH 13TH, 1918

"Last night was the same. The Germans were relentless. However, on the third night, they must have thought we would give up. They hit us with a gas attack, followed by the heaviest artillery barrage I have ever been in to make it worse. They were deadly accurate. They must have had a spotter within yards of us. Shells rained down on the trenches and in the rear near the supplies. I couldn't imagine the destruction the shells caused. But like the other nights, their infantry advanced, and we drove them back with machine gun fire and artillery. They come in waves, one after another. I don't know how they can sustain losses like this every day. I even threw a couple of hand grenades. I must have hit someone because, after my last hand grenade, the shelling stopped."

MARCH 15TH, 1918

"Spring is in the air. The trenches are no longer frozen. Now, they are just muddy, and the stench is overwhelming. There must be three inches of water on the floor with more inches of mud underneath it. There is mud everywhere. The mud is unlike any other I have seen. It sticks to everything and is almost impossible to remove when it dries. It's strange that you can

hear the birds back home when it's springtime, but not here. The only thing I hear is the rats feeding on the dead soldiers' corpses. Some of them are as big as cats."

MARCH 18TH, 1918

"I had KP duty yesterday. All the damage caused by the attack the other night was gone. I enjoyed the break. I have never peeled so many potatoes or opened more cans of meat. But with a nip in the air, it was nice to be around the stoves and fires. I got to know some of the cooks. One guy was from New York City. I could hardly understand him when he talked, but damn, he could cook. He told me he would open 'Totonno Pizzeria' after the war. I replied, 'Well, if you do, and if I'm ever in New York City, I will stop in for a pizza.' He saw me writing in my diary between peeling potatoes and opening cans during a bit of downtime. He asked me, 'What are you writing about?' I told him about Totonno Pizzeria. He slapped me on the back and said in the thickest Italian accent, 'For you, free pizza for life.'

The other day, a couple of soldiers and I were assigned to a new unit. They were short a few men, so I volunteered to join them. The soldier I'm writing the letters for volunteered, too. He said, 'He didn't know who else would write his letters.' Even though he is doing very well in his writing, he wants to be with someone he knows and can trust immediately."

MARCH 29TH, 1918

"I was part of another raiding party with my new unit. Only a few of us were there, but we caught the Germans off guard. We left in the middle of the night, crawled through their wire, and waited till sunrise. The officer with us saw their sentinel and motioned us to get into the trench. We had the advantage of surprise. We leaped up and jumped into their trench. We overran their position before they knew what hit them. As I grabbed one of the German officers, I pulled out my pistol and pointed it at him. Suddenly, he said in perfect English, 'I'm an American officer. Don't shoot me.' I just looked at him and pulled the hammer back on my .45 cal pistol. I replied, 'Sure you are, Fritz, now get down.' I put the pistol at the base of his skull. He said, 'I

work for military intelligence. My name is Allen Dulles. Have your lieu-tenant verify it. I'm going to put my right hand in my left jacket pocket. Don't shoot!' He pulled out a small card and handed it to me. 'Here, give him this name.' I called over the lieutenant and told him the German's story. He took the card and said, 'Get up, Allen, and come with us.'

We captured a few of them and brought them back with us. The rest of them lay dead in the trench, some face up and some face down. We, however, all made it out and back to our trench alive."

MARCH 30TH, 1918

"I ran into the lieutenant from the other night, and he said, 'I'm lucky I didn't kill the German; he was an American, after all.' I looked at him and asked, 'A spy?'

He smiled and walked off."

CHAPTER 10

BACK TO THE REAR

Walter had a surprise for Alex today. After breakfast, they got in their rental car and drove out of Paris on their way to Gisors, only sixty-two kilometers away. With traffic, Walter hoped to be there by mid-morning, but he hadn't told Alex where they were headed yet. The area around Gisors was considered the rear, even though it was only seventy-five kilometers from the Montdidier front. Troops would arrive by train or truck for training and preparing for open combat.

"So, Dad, where are we going?" Alex asked.

"I did a little research after you went to bed last night and found a place near Paris we should visit. The town is Gisors, a beautiful and ancient town. It was used back in the war as a place for troops to reorganize, replenish supplies, train, and rest. We still do that in the modern Army. Troops must come off the line at some point; when, and how long or how often depends on your mission and the situation."

"Wow, I'm impressed. How much farther?"

"Maybe an hour or ninety minutes, depending on traffic."

As they drove, Alex stared out the window and admired France's beautiful countryside, with rolling hills and green fields. With clear skies and a temperature in the mid-sixties, it was a perfect day for a road trip. He looked at his dad, smiled, and said, "Are we there yet?"

He grinned. "Some things never change, and not yet."

Alex took out the diary and started reading.

APRIL 4TH, 1918

"At last, we came off the front the other day. We are in a rear area for training and resupply, which is good. I need some new boots and socks. All my other equipment is in good shape. I really like the unit I was assigned to. They are a great bunch of guys as we got off the trucks by the rail station. Trains passed without slowing down, filled with soldiers from Britain and France moving toward the front. I know it won't be long until we are with them, but I will enjoy being in the rear for now. As I watched the trains go by, I noticed all the soldiers had the same look on their faces as we did when we moved to the front. One of determination, pride, and knowing this may be their last day alive."

APRIL 10TH, 1918

"The training has been challenging and rigorous. The officers and NCOs continually point out what we did wrong when we were on the front and what we did well. We spend a lot of time in our gas masks. I still haven't figured out how to get a drink of water while wearing one. Some guys hold their breath, break the seal, and take a gulp of water. I don't take it off until I hear the all-clear signal.

Yesterday, we held a brigade formation, and the unit received an award from the French army in recognition of our actions during our time on the front. After the formation, the morale in the division was as high as any unit I have ever been in. There is a renewed sense of pride. The weeks we spent on the front and seeing our fellow soldiers die took a lot out of us. The twenty-four-hour sounds of war and its consequences weigh heavily on most of us. It reminds me of this poem by Sir Herbert Read:"

The Happy Warrior
His wild heart beats with painful sobs,
His strain'd hands clench an ice-cold rifle,
His aching jaws grip a hot parch'd tongue,
His wide eyes search unconsciously.
He cannot shriek.
Bloody saliva
Dribbles down his shapeless jacket.
I saw him stab
And stab again
A well-killed Boche.
This is the happy warrior,
This is he...

APRIL 15TH, 1918

"We have almost finished our training. The unit was allowed some time to spend in the local town. After spending so much time on the front and training for open combat, it's hard to relax. I feel I'm always on. I can't turn myself off. However, yesterday was a great day. The major difference between here and the front was not the absence of gunfire or artillery blasts, nor the constant fear of gas attacks; it was that flowers were growing. These beautiful flowers, which I took for granted throughout my entire life, have now given me a new perspective on life. I wanted to touch and smell each one when I ran my hand over them. The softness of the pedals and blooms was therapeutic.

The smiles on the faces of the citizens were contagious. This town has not been spared the ravages of war. Many of its citizens have been killed or disfigured, but somehow, they moved forward. I hope one day I can do the same. Death and killing are two things I want to put in the deepest part of my mind when the war is over—going to lock it away and throw away the key. I stopped at a local bakery, and the pastries were excellent. I ate three of them. The coffee tasted so good that I didn't add any sugar or milk. I found a park bench nestled between two trees. There were already a couple of soldiers from the unit sitting on it. I walked over and sat down on the end. No one said a word. There was no need for words. We all knew what each other was thinking, and we all had smiles. We just sat there basking in the sun and consuming as much of the scent of the flowers as we could. After an hour or so, we all got up and returned to the barracks, again not saying a word."

"Son, we are almost there," Walter said.

Alex closed the diary. "Dad, why did you pick this place?"

"I thought it would be a great place to see what the soldiers did when not on the front. After all, they were in constant combat. Everyone needs a break. How about we leave the diary in the car and enjoy the town like our unknown soldier did?"

"Dad, I have to say, you're on a roll with great ideas."

They got out of the car. Alex walked over to his dad, put his arm around him, and said, "I owe you."

Smiling from ear to ear, Walter said, "You owe me nothing. I'm your father. Now, if you want to buy lunch, I'm good with that."

Alex took his arm off his father's shoulder, patted him on his back, and said, "Sounds good, and you can even pick the place." They headed toward the center of town side by side, father and son walking as one.

After spending time in Gisors, they got back in the car. Walter had another surprise for Alex. They weren't returning to Paris but to where the war raged in April 1918.

Gisors was just the beginning of a day Alex would never forget.

CHAPTER 11

THE SALIENT

VILLERS-TOURNELLE, FRANCE

The weather was still holding up, and the traffic was light as they drove to the vicinity of Villers-Tournelle, France. Before rereading it, Alex pulled out the diary and asked, "What did you like about the Army? From what I'm reading in the diary, it seems all they did was train. He doesn't talk much about the relationships he forged. I remember you always talking about the folks you met in the Army."

"Well, he did mention a couple. Remember the soldier he wrote the letters for and the cook. For some reason, he's not mentioning names or places. I think he was more worried about what would happen if the Germans got hold of his diary—now, getting back to your original question. What I loved about the Army was that everyone looked out for one another and focused on the mission at hand. The fellowship, esprit de corps, and if you did your job and obeyed the rules, you could advance, regardless of color, sex, religion, or where you were from."

Alex opened it and continued to read.

APRIL 18TH, 1918

"Well, our time in the rear area is ending. I feel rested, relaxed, and ready, albeit with some hesitation, to move back to the front. The war still has to be fought, and I'm ready for the fight. My gear is packed, and my weapon is cleaned and loaded. The trucks are all lined up. They aren't for us. We are infantry. We walk!"

APRIL 23RD, 1918

"We are back on the march. I've been at it for a couple of days. Yesterday, we took a break from marching, and I had time to take my pack off and lean against it. It weighs over fifty pounds, and I felt like I was floating when I took it off. I closed my eyes for a few minutes until I heard the noise from above. I opened my eyes and counted at least fifteen planes, our planes, flying toward the northwest. I could almost feel the vibrations from all the engines. What magnificent machines. I could tell they were our planes by the paint scheme and the different markings on the aircraft. American planes feature a roundel of three concentric circles: a red outer circle, a blue middle circle, and a white inner circle. The Germans have a black cross. During our training, they showed us pictures of German, French, British, and American planes so that we could identify them. We don't want to shoot at the wrong plane. It didn't take long for them to fly by. They go faster than anything I have seen. Once they were gone, I closed my eyes and saw myself flying one and how free it must feel—flying like a bird, flying through the clouds and reaching out to touch them. My brown leather flight jacket and matching helmet, goggles, and white scarf fluttered in the air—the sound of the motor and the feel of it vibrating through the plane, basking in the freedom.

Then, all of a sudden, I see a German plane above me. I add power to the engine to meet my opponent and position myself in a match to the death. I maneuver my plane behind the German airplane, getting into a dogfight (which is when two planes fight each other in the air). He can't escape my skills as a pilot. I get closer behind him and pull the machine gun triggers, seeing the rounds impact the enemy plane, watching as it goes down in flames, and then flying close to the ground and rejoicing over my kill. Then, I will fly back to the airfield and sleep in a bed in a warm room, not a muddy trench. The war has changed me ..."

APRIL 25TH, 1918

"Well, after a few long days of marching. I'm at the front again. Strangely, it feels good. Almost back to where I belong. I spent the first part of the day digging a dugout for the company commander. I helped lay some telephone lines, ensured the trenches' berm was high enough, and reinforced the wooden beams that provided us a little protection from shelling. Every once in a while, I could hear an artillery shell impacting in front of the trench. I think it was just to let us know they were still out there. Well, for one, I never forgot.

While assisting in digging the dugout, I saw the battle map. The Germans were on all three sides of us. As I looked at it, one of the lieutenants walked over and showed me where we were located. We are pretty damn close to the Germans. Once they attack, we won't have much time to prepare, taking a look at what was on the map. A couple of divisions of Germans were on the other side of No man's land.

When I returned to my position, the word came down the line that our mission was to hold the line. The Germans can't, under any circumstances, break through the line, and we are expecting an attack at any time. Everyone was ready. I needed to change my boots, but before I did, I rechecked my rifle and ammo. I even put a couple of grenades in my small dugout. At least the weather is getting nice. There's a little rain, but it's getting warmer. The trenches are still a muddy, wet, miserable place. I return to what the French trainers said, 'Trenches are hell on earth.' I can't fully illustrate how lousy life is in the trenches: rats everywhere, lice, mud on every piece of your clothes and equipment. The smell of mildew is everywhere. No individual space, constant noise, and soldiers running by you. I guess that is why I volunteered for another raiding party tonight. It gets me out of this miserable place. When I return home, I will never get in another hole or ditch."

April 27th, 1918

"Last night, I went on another raid with a squad from my platoon. Our mission was not to kill, but kill I did. We want to capture them. We need information on their intent to ensure our defenses are properly set up. Before we started the raid, the squad leader said to stay out of the ravines along the road we would cross. Mustard gas is still persistent in them. I wonder how long the gas will continue to pose a threat. Will it last after the war?

We exited our trench, and in front of us was that road. It was a full moon, but luckily, it was overcast, so we all ran and jumped over the ravines. Once we crossed the road, we crouched and moved quickly to a location along their line where the defenses were less, based on a reconnaissance flight by one of our planes the previous afternoon. We could infiltrate them much more easily than we thought, even from the reconnaissance flight. We found a spot where there was almost no wire. Once in the trench, we discovered a telephone line and followed it to a dugout, which was guarded by only one soldier. I moved along the wall of the trench. As I was moving on him, the artillery barrage started, and shells landed behind us. As the shells impacted, he turned, and I was face-to-face with him. Before he had a chance to yell or sound the alarm, I put my left hand over his mouth, and in my right hand was my trench knife. I plunged it into his chest, killing him. I stabbed him in the same place where those red dots on the dummies were. I held on to him, lowered him to the ground, and pulled my knife out. The squad leader moved over to him and entered the communication dugout. As he was moving in, I cut the telephone line. So, any communication he was going to send went nowhere. I could hear the battle going on in the dugout. My mission was to watch down the trench and stop any German soldiers coming out or trying to get in. I had my pistol at the ready.

After three or four minutes, the squad emerged with five German prisoners from the dugout. I was in the rear, with my pistol out. We didn't carry any rifles for the mission. We each had our trench knives, pistols, and two hand grenades. We arrived at the entry point, where we used to enter their trench. The artillery had stopped. The squad leader took his flare gun out and fired a flare, indicating to our lines that we were about to make our way back to our trenches. All of us were out of the trench and crawling to our line when all of a sudden, one of the German soldiers jumped and yelled,

"Amerikanische Soldaten!" American Soldiers. Before he could repeat it, the German machine guns opened up, killing him. When the German machine guns opened up, ours started firing soon after. We all huddled in an artillery crater. Dirt and water flew in the air all around us, and the ground under me vibrated. The air tasted like gunpowder. The tracer rounds were going over my head from both directions as our machine guns opened up. Finally, the fire stopped on both sides. We crawled out of the crater and made our way to our lines.

We took the prisoners to the command post and returned to our sector on the line. I took off my gear and sat down on an ammo box. I looked down, and my hands were trembling, and I started to sweat. The next thing I knew, a soldier was standing over me. 'Hey, you okay? It looks like you got some shrapnel in your arm. I put a bandage around it.'

I thanked him and fell asleep."

MAY 1ST, 1918

"My arm is all healed. It wasn't much of a wound. The Germans are continuing their artillery attacks. The only thing that has changed is that they are now hitting more of the surrounding areas to our rear and in the local villages. There are so many troops here that some support soldiers must stay in the villages. It makes them easy targets. I'm going out on patrol tonight and looking forward to getting out of the trench to retrieve our wounded and dead. There has been so much shelling that we can only go and get out wounded and bring back the dead at night. You can hear the screaming of the wounded. Everyone sounds different. Sometimes, you can hear the wounded Germans. They can't get theirs till dark, either. I hope I can get a German as a prisoner. We take care of them just as we would our soldiers. There is still some civility in war."

MAY 5TH, 1918

"The other night was the most intense artillery attack with a mix of high explosives and mustard gas. It was a perfect night for a gas attack with no wind. The cloud of gas just hovered. I had my gas mask on for hours till the

gas cloud dissipated. The soldiers on the front were spared. However, the support soldiers took the brunt of the attack and were not as well-trained in donning their gas masks. I heard a rumor there were over eight hundred casualties from the shelling and the gas attack."

MAY 7TH, 1918

"The Germans switched from shelling the rear to shelling the front. Shells hit all around me and my platoon. The ground shook constantly. At the same time, shells rained down on us. They opened up with machine gun fire. By the wall of bullets, every machine gun must have been firing. The bullets were impacting behind me. They hit a wooden sign, and it looked like Swiss cheese when the firing was over. I heard a soldier down the line from me screaming. I ran over there, and he had been hit in the shoulder. I pulled his shirt back to look at the wound. It went in and out of his shoulder. I removed his first aid pack and applied a bandage to stop the bleeding. You always use the first aid pack of the soldier you're treating. I dusted the wound with sulfa and gave him a couple of tablets to fight the infection till a stretcher-bearer or doctor could attend to him. I told him to keep pressure on the wound. It was bleeding, but not from an artery. I helped him up and took him to the casualty clearing station. When I arrived, I couldn't believe how many soldiers were waiting to be seen. In a group of them, I noticed one of the soldiers was already dead. The doctors, stretcher bearers, and medical staff were working as fast as they could, and at the same time, doing a great job. There were just not enough of them after the attack the other night. The damage the German machine guns can do to a body is catastrophic. Many of the soldiers were hit more than once.

I had to leave. There was nothing I could do, and I was more worried about a German attack. When I got back to my station, our artillery started shelling the German positions. It was getting dark. I could see the light from the artillery cannons in the distance. It looked like lightning. Then, the Germans counterfired our artillery. I could barely make out when their guns fired, but after a minute, I could see their shells impacting in front of me. When the explosions from the shell landed, the sky looked like the sun rising —a beautiful, reddish-orange sky that was almost mesmerizing. I started to count how long it took from the flash until I heard the bang: one thousand, one thousand, two, and so on. Each second was a mile, so if I counted to three, that meant that potential death was three miles in front of me and, with each volley, was getting closer. We must have fired hundreds of shells. I didn't think the Germans would attack after that barrage, and they didn't. They must have many wounded to attend to. There is so much shelling and gunfire. One of these days, there will be just two soldiers left. I am sure they would look around and say, Why?"

May 15th, 1918

"I was selected to go out with artillery soldiers yesterday at dawn. There were four of us. We exited the trench and crawled about three hundred yards. We set up an observation post in a large crater, providing us with a clear field of vision to monitor the Germans. I was assigned a new weapon, a BAR. It's heavier than my normal rifle, but boy, can it put rounds down range and a lot of them. One of the other soldiers had a spool of telephone wire, allowing the forward observer to communicate with his artillery battery.

Once we're all set up, the FO gave his battery some grid coordinates of the Germans. When he was done, I could hear the sound of the cannons firing. Within a matter of seconds, I saw the shells impacting. Once the first volley was completed, the FO made some adjustments, and within another few seconds, more and more shells struck the Germans. After the barrage had finished, we started to receive mortar fire and machine guns. With our mission complete, we abandoned the OP and returned to our trench. While we moved back, one of the soldiers was hit by machine guns and died right next to me. I grabbed him by his equipment straps and pulled him into the trench. I would not leave a soldier for the rats to dine on."

May 23rd, 1918

"I have spent the last few days out of the trenches. It felt good. I got some great sleep and played some poker. I'm not very good, since we can't carry money around, and I only lost some pride. Rumor has it that we will be coming off the line for a while. I don't know why, but there is a rumor that

something big is about to happen. By the way, the Army lives on rumors. I do have some good news. I got promoted to corporal the other day. I was not expecting it, but my platoon sergeant said I deserved it. So, now I'm a squad leader. I hope I make the right decisions and can lead my men proudly. After getting promoted, I prayed for strength and my men."

They drove past Villers-Tournelle to Cantigny. "Hey, Dad, why are we going to Cantigny?"

Walter looked at him. "This is the first place the American Army launched a divisional offensive against the Germans. The 1st Infantry Division was under French control. The area we just passed is where they trained for the attack."

Walter parked the car near the Cantigny American Monument, which is located in the city park. They both got out. Alex put the diary in his backpack and slung it over his shoulder. Walking up to the monument, Alex felt like something was pushing him. He looked around, and there was nothing. He shrugged it off. When they got to the monument, the feeling subsided.

As they looked out, Walter said, "See how beautiful the terrain looks now. Back then, it must have been a wasteland. Just think of opposing armies facing each other in a death match."

"Dang, this is pretty cool."

Walter could hear the excitement in his son's voice.

"Well, the day has just started. Come on, let's go."

"Hold on, Dad. Here, take a picture of me next to the monument."

Walter took Alex's phone and snapped a photo. "Here, take a look at it before we go."

Alex looked at the picture and texted his mom. He received a reply quickly.

"Son, you look great! How is the trip? I didn't want to disturb you guys."

Alex texted back.

"The trip is awesome. Dad is great!"

He put his phone back in his pocket, glanced at his father, and smiled.

"What are you smiling at?"

"Nothing, Dad."

As they returned to their car, Alex put his arm around his dad and smiled—no words needed to be said.

As Walter pulled out of the parking lot, he asked, "How about we go down to the area they fought in?"

"Now, that would be cool."

Walter pointed the car toward Fontaine-sous-Montdidier. He turned right at the fork in the road and stopped at the American First Division Stelae. They exited the car and walked toward it.

Alex remembered leaving the diary in the car, so he returned and grabbed it. As he neared the Stelae, that strange feeling returned. This time, it was one of anguish. He didn't say anything to his dad, though.

The names of the 1138 members of the division who gave their lives in the local area are on the Stelae. His dad pointed to the wood line down the hill and said, "Right down there was the nearest American line. This is where the first offensive American attack occurred."

"But Dad, in the diary, he talked about being in battle before the date on the monument."

"Son, you're a hundred percent correct. However, he mentioned either an attack from Germany or the raids he went on. Now, what that combat did was season the soldiers. Come on, we have more to explore today."

They got back in the car and drove to their next stop. They went through Mensil-Saint-Georges onto Villiers-Tournelle. Villers-Tournelle was under constant artillery attack since it was a communications hub for the French and Americans. After visiting the battle area, a medical company was housed in the village.

"Alex, just think about this. There were thousands of soldiers on both sides of the front, each one wanting to kill the other. The Americans came out of the trenches and ran into a wall of bullets. As they ran, their fellow soldiers would fall around them. Once they got into mortar range, those shells would fall on them, yet they continued to move forward. They would dive into shell craters and find maybe a German soldier already there, dead."

"It's so brutal when you think about it, yet they did what they were ordered to do. I don't know if I could do that."

"Son, they were soldiers, and that's what soldiers do. They follow orders and trust their fellow soldiers to do their job. That's why soldiers train daily. It becomes muscle memory, and you react without thinking." Walter stared off at nothing for a moment. "Well, son, I hope you never have to find out, though. Come on, let's get back to Paris."

They walked back to the car. Once inside, Walter pulled out of the parking lot. They'd be back at the hotel in an hour or so.

Alex dozed off soon after they got on the road.

As he slept, the words of the unknown soldier came to life in his dreams.

CHAPTER 12

GOING ON THE OFFENSIVE

LEAVING: VILLERS-TOURNELLE, FRANCE

Alex woke up and looked out at the countryside. In his mind, he envisioned the shells impacting the field as the soldiers ran toward the enemy. He could almost see the faces of the soldiers, the steadfast determination in their eyes. A look he had seen in his father's eyes when he returned from a deployment. Now he knew why. He closed his eyes for a brief moment and asked himself if he'd ever be as brave as the unknown soldier or his dad. He opened his eyes and stared out the window at the farms and fields. After a minute or two, he opened the diary and started reading.

MAY 24TH, 1918

"I knew it was too good to be true. As soon as my squad and I got comfortable, we packed up and marched to a new location. We have been attacking trenches and positions that are exactly like the Germans'. I mean everything. I guess some of the prisoners coughed up some information. My squad has been doing a great job, so we have been selected to lead the simulated attack every iteration and take out their machine gun nests. I'm proud

of my men. They are a great bunch of fellas. The good thing about being the squad leader is that I no longer have to carry the BAR. It got heavy quickly.

I was standing in a trench; the ground shook, and the noise was unfamiliar. There was no artillery. I couldn't figure out what was going on until I got on a wooden box and looked over to my right, and there, crawling across No-man's-land was a huge steel vehicle on some tracks. They call it a tank. It wasn't fast, but I don't see how it can be stopped. It even had a tube protruding from the front of it. I didn't know what it was until it went bang, and a fireball and smoke came out of it. It fired a huge bullet, a cannon of some sort. The ground trembled again. There were three more. It was amazing to watch them drive over the trenches. I was so focused on the tanks that I didn't hear the whistle to move out of the trench and attack. My platoon sergeant came up behind me and kicked me in the butt and told me to pull my head out.

I looked down the line at my squad and motioned for them to attack. My foot slipped in the mud as I climbed out of the trench. Another soldier was right behind me. He put his hand on my butt and pushed me over the berm. My squad climbed out of our trench and ran across the field. As we moved, we fired on the simulated machine gun nest. As we got closer, I motioned for the squad to take cover and threw our hand grenades. When there is no one firing back at you, the task of taking out a machine gun nest is much, much easier.

After the mission, my platoon sergeant called me over and chewed my ass. One that I won't forget anytime soon. He said, 'I'd better start acting like an NCO, or I'm going to get all my men killed.' I can't let that happen. I gathered my squad and told them I failed them today, but it won't happen again. I took them to the back of the trenches, and we practiced repeatedly. We reviewed everyone's roles and responsibilities. I even made sure everyone knew each other's mission. Just in case someone gets hit, we can still complete our task. Once everyone was satisfied, we could complete our mission. We sat around and relaxed for the remainder of the time. One of the squad members even came up and thanked me for drilling them so hard. I might make a good NCO after all."

Alex stopped reading. "Dad, have you ever gotten your butt chewed by another NCO?"

Walter didn't take his eyes off the road. "Well, there's one time that stands out. I was a Spec 4 and drove the brigade deputy commander and the command sergeant major. Like every day, I got up, put my uniform on, and went to work. As I walked up the stairs in the brigade headquarters, the CMS said, 'Specialist, your shirt collar is torn. You need to go and change your shirt.' I replied that I was not returning to the barracks to change my shirt. Now, don't ask me why I said that. It was the dumbest thing I could have said. After about one second, he replied, 'Get your ass in my office. Now!"

"Hold on, Dad. Did you say that to a command sergeant major? Even I know not to say that."

"I was young. Let me finish. I walked into his office, which I have been in numerous times. I walked to his desk, and before I could stop him, he said, 'Get to parade rest and don't say one word.' As I was standing there, he went up one side of me and down the other, never raising his voice. He said, 'If you ever talk like that to me again, your ass is grass, and I'm a lawn mower. Now get your ass to the barracks and change your damn shirt. Get out of here and have the jeep out front in ten minutes. If I were you, I would double time. Don't be late. Dismissed.' I didn't say a word. I did an about-face and ran out of his office, and well, I was pretty fast back then. I had the Jeep in the back of the headquarters in nine minutes, wearing a new shirt. He got in the jeep and said, 'Specialist, let's go to the flight line.' He never said another word about the incident. I learned a lot about leadership that day. Never hold a grudge. If you do, it ruins the cohesiveness of a unit and morale."

"Is that why you never stayed mad at me for doing stupid stuff?"

"No, I stayed mad." Walter laughed.

"Are we there yet?"

Now, they both laughed like they hadn't laughed in years. The diary was bringing them closer.

Alex opened it and continued to read.

"After chow, the platoon got together and reviewed some drawings from the reconnaissance airplanes. This, combined with the information gathered from prisoners, provides a fairly clear picture of what we will be up against, and it's not a pretty one. They are dug in and have a defense in depth, meaning many layers of trenches, wires, obstacles, and machine gun emplacements."

MAY 25TH, 1918

"Today, we spent all day working with the French tanks. They move pretty slowly, so keeping up with them is not hard. We started the day with some of the tanks we would work with in the upcoming mission. First, they showed us the inside of one of the tanks. From the outside, it looked like there was plenty of room. However, once they started to show us the inside, it would be cramped with a full crew of thirteen. It looked a little cramped, and with the engine on, there was a lot of smoke. After the inside, we moved around the outside, and they gave some details. The tank is called the Char 2C. They pointed out what they call a turret. This is where the 75 mm main weapon is located, and it can turn. It allows the tank to shoot targets on the right or left. Not only did it have the main weapon, but it also had four machine guns. They told us it could cross a trench that is twelve feet wide. I want to drive one of these, but we will be behind it, on its left, or on its right as we move on to the objective. After seeing the French tank, I can't wait to see the tanks we have."

MAY 26TH, 1918

"Today, we moved up to the front lines. We took our positions and immediately verified that everyone knew who was on their left and right. I had each squad member check their ammo and prepare for the upcoming mission. It was still daylight, so we had a good field of view, and the drawing and all the intelligence we received were one hundred percent correct. I walked the line to make sure we were ready. When I was done, I sat down, prayed for my soldiers, and asked for guidance and the strength to make the right decisions. I want to be the leader they deserve. Occasionally, the Germans would fire

several artillery shells. With every volley getting closer to our position, just when I thought they would unleash all their guns, they went silent. Once it got dark, I put the squad on a rotation, half on duty, the other half getting rest or chow and switching every four hours."

MAY 27TH, 1918

"Early this morning, the Germans unleashed a fierce barrage of artillery on the line of trenches before mine. Dirt was rising thirty to forty feet in the air. The shells would land in a crater filled with water every so often. You could see a rainbow when the water shot up at a right angle against the sun. It's crazy what you notice with death looking you right in the eyes.

As lethal as the artillery is, it was a fantastic sight. This was just in preparation for one of their raiding parties. When the artillery barrage lifted, they were able to penetrate our trenches. The fighting was intense and fierce in the trenches, but our troops prevailed. I have never seen men fight the way they did in the attack. It was hand-to-hand combat in the trenches, Germans too close to kill with rifles or pistols. The sound of metal hitting against metal was heard as the soldiers used bayonets and trench knives to fight. The brutality of hand-to-hand combat."

"Hey, Dad, look at his writing about hand-to-hand combat. It looks like his hand was shaking." Alex held up the diary for his father to see.

"Yes, it sure does. He is under a tremendous amount of stress. Easy tasks become very difficult, and decision-making can become impaired. That is a good catch, son."

"During the hand-to-hand combat, I saw utter evil in one of my soldiers. The look in his eyes was hollow and dark. He had just stabbed one of the German soldiers. The soldier fell to the ground, bleeding out. The soldier raised his knife and continued to stab him over and over. Even though he was dead. I ran over and grabbed his arm. He turned to me with his knife raised as if he were going to stab me. I pushed him back. His eyes met mine.

They were fully open and not blinking. I yelled, 'Soldier, soldier, put the knife down.' He looked at me with eyes of nothingness, an emptiness, a void of humanity. Another soldier ran up behind him and hit him in the back of the head with his rifle, knocking him out. My heart was pumping faster and faster. We were still fighting the Germans in the trench, and I was one soldier down.

A German soldier jumped into the trench just feet from me. I grabbed the trench knife from the soldier who was down and made a lunging move toward the German. He moved to my right and slashed my forearm. I jumped back, took out my pistol, and pulled the trigger. The bullet hit him in the center of his forehead. He dropped to the ground. I searched his pockets and pulled out his military papers. As I put his papers in my pocket, my hands were trembling. I tried to stop the trembling, but couldn't. He was the last German soldier in their attack, and he was dead. I killed him.

After the attack, bayonets and trench knives were dripping with the blood of the German soldiers who lay on the floor. The German bayonets also had the blood of American soldiers dripping from them. Our soldiers fought with so much tenacity that the attack was repelled within hours. Dead bodies from both the Germans and Americans littered the floor of the trench. The Germans who didn't flee were captured. My squad captured three German soldiers, but our units were not spared in the attack. An engineer unit assigned to us took substantial casualties as the Germans breached our perimeter.

There was no time to dwell on our success. I heard the whistle to prepare for a counterattack. I stopped worrying about my trembling hands. I was a soldier and did what soldiers had done for thousands of years. Kill their enemy. Before we exited the trench, our artillery started firing. They must have fired hundreds of shells. As I climbed out of the trench, a soldier next to me was fully exposed as he came out of the trench. He was cut down by machine gun fire. I continued to move, and I didn't have time to mourn. As we made our way to the German lines, there was no machine gun fire, only some sporadic artillery shelling or mortar fire. When we got to the German lines, the trenches were empty of living beings. Only dead soldiers remained. The rest must have escaped to fight another day. Among the dead was a captured French soldier. One I recognized from my training. I had a couple of men from my squad pick him up and carry him back to our lines. He was going to get a proper burial.

After the attack and our counterattack, I went back, and the soldier was still unconscious. I got some water and threw it on him, waking him up. He looked at me and asked, 'What the hell happened?' He then started to cry. I didn't tell him. I could see he was in pain; it was not physical but more mental. I got a couple of my soldiers and had them escort him back to the stretcher-bearers. He needed help, but I couldn't give it to him. The front was no place for him. He gave it all without being killed. He had the 1000-yard stare. I hate war."

"Hey, Dad, what is the 1000-yard stare?"

"It was a term they used in WWI, WWII, the Korean War, and the Vietnam War. It has to do with a blank stare. Today, they call it Post Traumatic Stress Disorder, commonly called PTSD. For soldiers, it can be caused by a traumatic, shocking, or terrifying incident."

"Do all soldiers get it? Do you have it?"

"I don't know if all soldiers have it. Some cases are more severe than others and sometimes require some therapy. A lot is kept bottled up until … well. I didn't want to admit it for a long time, but yes, I did. I think it was one reason your mom and I got divorced. She tried to help, but I pushed her back. I thought I could take care of it myself. Now, I talk to other veterans, and there are a lot of support groups."

"Damn, Dad, I didn't know. What can I do? Please let me know."

"Son, you're doing it."

They sat in silence for a while.

"Dad, mind if I continue reading?"

"Please continue. I'm all ears."

MAY 28TH, 1918

"Today, we go on the offensive. There will be little time for rest or sleep. My squad has been selected to advance and establish firing positions in the shell craters outside our perimeter. We have some French flamethrowers

attached to the platoon. I have yet to see them in action, but I can imagine what they can do to a person. This battle will be different. We are going to rid a village of the Germans. It will be house-to-house fighting, the most dangerous. Finally, out of the trenches, not for sure that is a good thing. There is fear in my men's eyes. I won't let them see mine."

MAY 29TH, 1918

"We established a couple of firing positions. Once we secured the area, we were relieved by another squad from a different platoon. We were ordered to leave the French flamethrowers at the firing positions. I was told we won't need them. We are returning to the trenches."

JUNE 4TH, 1918

"I'm exhausted! Over the last few days, the combat has been the bloodiest and most brutal I have ever been involved in. The French tanks moved into position before the order was given to advance over the trenches. They were positioned to our rear, between my trench and the one behind us. They put some material, I think steel, to build a bridge over the trench so they could cross it quickly. Damn, they are so impressive. I know they have to give us some advantage. I know the Germans have them, too, but I haven't seen theirs, and I hope I don't.

The first day of the attack was hazy and sticky. It turned out to be damn hot. The artillery and mortars had been firing on the town well before we left the security of the trench. As we waited for the signal to assault, I peered over the trench berm and saw the punishment the artillery was inflicting on the village. Buildings crumbled from the direct hits and the concussions from the shells surrounding them. In the pre-dawn, the sky lit up like a burnt orange tint, flames and debris reaching high into the air, raining down on the German fortifications. I know there were screams and chaos in the village, but I couldn't hear the screams or see the chaos.

I was focused on the mission at hand. I got off my wooden box and walked down the line in the mud. It had yet to dry out. I don't think it ever will. At each one of my soldiers, I stopped and made them check their weapons and ammo, fix bayonets, and ensure each one had their gas mask. I reiterated what our mission was and told them to stay focused. One soldier said, 'Yes, Corporal, the sooner we get them out of the town, the sooner I can be back to mine.' We prayed together. As he got up, I patted him on the back and gave him a thumbs-up. What we didn't know at the time was that he would be killed in the assault. He is going back to his town after all.

I looked at the sky, and the wind had shifted toward the town. I yelled to my squad to get their gas masks at the ready. No more than one minute later, the gas alarm sounded. Everyone put on their mask. It wouldn't be long before we faced the enemy again. This time, we are the attackers. I do know from my training that soldiers in the defense have at least a four-to-one chance of repelling an attack. I wasn't the only one who knew it. I could see on the faces of my men that they did, too.

While our artillery was pounding the Germans, the tanks moved out in front of the lines. I ordered my squad out of the trench and to get behind the tanks. It is magnificent to watch them move, then stop and fire. My platoon's mission was to move ahead and occupy some of the shell craters with our BAR. As my squad moved out of the trench, I looked up and could hear the sound of airplanes. I didn't know if they were ours or the Germans'. It didn't take long for me to know for sure, as the bombs fell from above. I have never seen such a thing.

I saw, off to my left, the results of the bombs dropped from the sky. Three dead American soldiers lay in positions that were not natural. I didn't have time to dwell on the deaths. I had to lead my squad. With the shelling continuing, we held our position outside of the town. There was very little return fire from the town.

After our artillery attack, I didn't see how anyone could be left alive in the town when the shelling stopped. After our artillery and the German air bombing, my squad moved into the town to mop up any Germans still alive. There were more German soldiers active and willing to die than anyone could have imagined.

We were still on the outskirts of the town when the German machine guns opened up. Soldiers to my left and right started to fall. I told my squad to get down and find cover. I glanced behind me and saw a mortar team begin to fire on the machine gun nest. I knew the rounds were going to be dangerously close. I told my squad to lie low and wait for my command to move forward. Just like I thought, the rounds started impacting right before my position. Even though they were the enemy, they were courageous soldiers. But one by one, they were being killed. I saw one building. It had a hole right through the brick and was still standing. I chuckled.

While the tanks continued the fight on the open ground, I ordered my squad to move into the village and start clearing operations as we entered the village's outskirts. In the near distance, I could hear the tanks firing, and suddenly I heard a muffled sound of multiple explosions. I looked over my shoulder to see where the sound came from. One of the French tanks had taken a direct hit from a German gun and was on fire. Flames were shooting out of the slits in the metal of the tank. The fire was causing the rounds in the tank to explode inside it. As I watched, I saw the side hatch open and the crew trying to get out. They were all on fire. I counted three that got out. Even though they were on fire and there was no way they would survive, the German machine guns found their targets and cut them to pieces. The others must have been trapped or killed by the explosions. I think they were the lucky ones. My heart sank. Never have I ever seen such carnage. This war never ceases to amaze me. God rest their souls.

The splattering of dirt on my face from German machine guns brought me back to the job at hand. I dropped to the ground and returned fire. I directed my squad to the house where the fire was coming from.

One of my soldiers ran up to the door of a house where we were receiving fire from the 3rd floor. He turned in the doorway and started firing. He then moved back against the door frame, and another soldier ran through the door and up the stairs. I followed him, and the remaining squad members were behind me. There was no resistance until we got to the third floor. That is when the gates of hell opened up on my squad. As soon as the first soldier made his way to the top of the stairs, a German was waiting there and shot him at point-blank range. My soldier got one shot off before falling to the floor, blood pouring out of his wound. As he lay on the floor, I heard the pain in his voice. 'Help me, Corporal, help me, help me.'

Everyone froze. We went back down one flight of stairs. Once there, I decided that another soldier and I would move slowly up the stairs. I took a grenade from my belt, pulled the pin, ran up the stairs, fell on the floor, and threw it into the room. The blast went over my body, but I could feel the concussion from the explosion. The soldiers behind me stormed up the stairs and into the room. They were face-to-face with two German soldiers with little life left in them. They opened up on them, hitting another of my men. The other soldier pulled out his pistol and shot both of them, ensuring they were dead. He took out his trench knife and stabbed each one in the heart.

The look on his face as he stabbed them was a look I saw in the French instructors. He crossed into the killing zone. The soldier would never be the same again. His world had just changed forever. By the time I got up off the floor, it was eerily quiet. I looked over to my soldier on the ground and started first aid. I was able to stop the bleeding by putting a tourniquet on his leg. What looked like a shot in his chest was, in reality, one to his upper leg. He was either extremely lucky, the German was a terrible shot, or he had a guardian angel looking over him. I dressed the wound. It looked to me like he would be okay. I walked over to another soldier. He wasn't so lucky. The Germans' bullets hit him multiple times in the chest. I fell to one knee. I looked up and yelled, 'Why, lord, why?' I took him by the hand and said, 'Soldier, you're going home. I think we will all be going home. I'm sorry.' I got up and said, 'Search the Germans.'

We searched the German soldiers and moved our wounded and our dead comrades out of the building. The rest of the village had been cleared when we exited the building. There were many captured Germans, but many, many more dead. They littered the streets and houses. They fought bravely, but they weren't up to the Americans.

Once we got out of the building, we laid the soldier on the ground. I knelt next to the body of the soldier I had talked to earlier in the day and prayed for him. I decided right then I would write the letter to his parents. I noticed then that I didn't cry. I don't feel empathy or sadness. I'm mad, I'm one soldier short in my squad.

Now we have to hold the village, and I heard the French artillery had to be reassigned toward Compiègne, where the Germans were mounting an offensive."

Alex shut the diary. "Dad, his demeanor has changed before my eyes. He's not the same man he was when he got to France."

"War will do that to you. The hotel is right around the corner. Let's get cleaned up, get dinner, and relax."

Alex didn't want to ask his dad how he had changed. Right now, his father was his entire world, and he'd learned so much about him on the trip.

"That sounds good," Alex said. "Maybe we can get some ice cream if I eat everything."

CHAPTER 13

RELENTLESS ARTILLERY

MARRIOTT HOTEL: PARIS, FRANCE

With only a couple of days left in France, Walter and Alex decided to drive to Compiègne and tour the private train car where the armistice was signed, marking the end of World War I. The private train car belonged to Marshal of France Ferdinand Foch.

"Hey, Dad, I'll read some while you're getting ready."

"Why don't you get ready first, and I'll read this morning?"

"Sounds great, but loud enough so I can hear it."

"Once the village was secure, we dug in and occupied it. With the French artillery."

"Dad, what date are you reading from?" Alex asked.

"The same day, June 4th, it is a continuation," he replied.

"Redeployed, the Germans took advantage of the reduction of counter-battery fire. They unleashed a torrent of shells. The ground shook, and buildings collapsed, soldiers screaming. Their counter-offensive wouldn't be far behind their shelling. During lulls in the shelling, machine-gun fire would open up, sending bullets toward any exposed soldiers. My squad took up a position just north of the building we cleared earlier. A soldier was with me in one position, with sandbags in front of us and the others in a shallow crater. We couldn't see the Germans, so we didn't fire our weapons. I had one of the soldiers run to the ammo point and get as many rounds as he could carry. When he returned, I sent him again to get ammo for the BAR.

Later in the afternoon, the German infantry advanced on our defensive positions on the southern and western sides. The unit to our south took the brunt of the attack. The attackers were quickly crushed by our artillery and machine-gun fire. One group of Germans broke through our defenses and was met by the French flame thrower. My god, the screams of the soldiers being burned alive were almost more than I could take. They ran down the street on fire, their arms flailing in the air, and then finally fell to the ground. The smell of the burning flesh is one I will never forget. I hope never to see the flamethrower in action again. I thought the gas attacks were bad.

With their fellow soldiers falling all around them, they continued attacking, and not one turned around. Only after running out of ammo did they retreat. They are a fierce fighting force. After years of fighting in the trenches, open fields, towns, and villages, they don't give up. At times, I admire their tenacity and bravery, but I want to kill as many as I can.

On the 30th, as the sun rose, they made their final attempt to reclaim the village. This time, my unit took the full force of their attack. They led again with artillery, then the infantry. A platoon of their infantry advanced toward my position. The sun rose, and I saw the sunlight bounce and reflect off one of their helmets. I yelled to my squad, 'Hold your fire. I repositioned myself a little farther up. As I moved, one of their machine guns opened up on me. I don't know how or why I was not hit. The rounds were impacting all around me on the street, off the building, and whizzing by my head.

I froze for a brief second and jumped behind a wall. When I did, the soldier with the BAR opened fire on the advancing infantry. Soldiers started dropping in front of me. I knelt behind the wall and fired my rifle. I took one *of my hand grenades and threw it. I could feel the blast through the wall. My head was ringing. I couldn't hear anything for a few minutes. The wall in front of me crumbled. There were only two tree stumps between the Germans and me, then fifty feet of open air. I fell to the ground. As I poked my head up, I saw mortar rounds hitting behind the advancing soldiers. As they ducked for cover, I got up and ran back toward my squad. When I got there, I was out of breath, and the soldier next to me said, 'I was as white as a ghost.' I had to pinch myself to make sure I wasn't a ghost. I rolled over, looked at the clear blue sky, and said, 'Thank you, lord.'*

The other members of my squad continued to fire at the retreating infantry. As I was watching what was unfolding to my front, I felt a tap on my shoulder. It was the platoon runner. My orders were to move forward, check the bodies, and treat the wounded. If there are any prisoners, gather them together and move them back. As he left, I could see the other squads advancing on the streets littered with dead and wounded soldiers. It looked like someone opened a potato sack and dumped bodies everywhere.

I heard the offensive was a success, and based on some prisoner intelligence, it affected the morale of the Germans. They felt defeated. Based on how many men we lost, if this were a success, I would hate to see a defeat."

JUNE 5TH, 1918

"Had very little sleep in the last few days. My squad was part of a raiding party last night. Artillery peppered the area with shelling, and we were able to get into their defensive positions and capture a couple of Germans. By the looks of them, they haven't been feeding them very well, and they both were injured. A stretcher-bearer could treat them once we got them back to our lines. One of the soldiers had a pretty nasty infection, and the stretcher-bearer treated him and the others. We then took them back to prisoner-holding areas. From there, I have no idea where they sent them."

JUNE 6TH, 1918

"Something is up. We are beefing up our bunkers and positions. Units are digging in the back of us. I guess in case we need to move back. Earlier in the day, I could hear airplanes flying. I looked up, and then the rest of my squad did the same. There were four planes in a dogfight. It looked like one of ours and three Germans. The beauty of the aerobatics and the skill of the pilots overshadowed the fact that they were in a fight to the death. As one tries to get into a position to kill the other. Being outnumbered, I didn't think the American pilot stood a chance. As I watched, the American plane swooped down and got behind one of the German planes. The German plane immediately dove toward the ground. The American plane followed him. The other two German planes took up positions behind the American plane. I could hear the whine of the engines and the fire of the machine guns, and see the tracers from the American plane impacting the German plane. Smoke started to come from the enemy plane, and we all stood up and cheered. The German plane descended toward the ground. We lost sight of it before we could see it impact the ground, surely killing the pilot.

The American plane pulled back up and, strangely enough, flew toward one of the German planes. As he got closer, they fired on each other, two knights on their flying horses in a jousting match to the death. The German plane was hit and began to smoke and dive to the ground. While the American pilot was firing on his opponent, the other German plane got into position behind him and opened fire. There was no maneuver he could perform to outmaneuver his stalker. Suddenly, he dove to the ground toward us. The enemy plane followed him, still firing its machine gun. It looked like he was going to crash into the earth when he pulled up and flew above the tops of the buildings in the village. The German was right behind him, continuing to fire. Black smoke poured out of our brave flyer's plane. I could hear the engine sputtering as the plane flew erratically. His wings went up and down as if waving at us. The German plane flew right over our heads, and as it did, we opened fire on it. I looked back toward the American plane but couldn't see it anymore. All I saw was smoke billowing from the tree line to the south of the village. The German plane pulled up and did what looked like a ballerina's pirouette, rejoicing at his kill.

A squad behind us was ordered to the crash site and retrieved the pilot's body. As they returned with his body, I knelt and prayed for the brave pilot.

It's been a long day. It's time to get some rest. I'm not the same man I was when I got here, nor are the other men in my squad. Death and destruction are an everyday occurrence."

June 9th, 1918

"I thought it stormed where we live. We had a thunderstorm last night that would rival any of our late spring storms. The sky was lit up by the light from spider lightning, cloud to cloud, and lightning striking the ground. It was the beauty of nature in full display. It was almost calming. At least no plane could or would fly in this weather. Heck, I thought artillery was coming down on us; it was so loud."

June 11th, 1918

"We moved back to the trenches last night. Another unit took up our position. Not a lot is going on right now. I have time to think, which is not a good thing. I would rather be busy. I'm going to volunteer for more raiding parties. It makes the time go quicker. I think I have lost around fifteen pounds. We only get one meal a day and have no water for cleaning. The morale is low up and down the ranks.

I had a dream last night. I could see all the faces in the dream, but not mine. I woke up, and my heart was racing. Maybe it was not a dream but a nightmare."

June 14th, 1918

"After a few days of intense fighting, some at a distance and some in close combat, we recaptured a major German stronghold. This will set up, I'm sure, a more significant offensive. My squad fought with courage. I'm so very proud of my soldiers. I find it an honor to call them my soldiers. I hope one day, when this is all over, we can all get together again and not have to worry about artillery, rifle fire, or bullets from machine guns, but most of all, gas.

The village we captured was a network of roads used to transport supplies to the Germans. My platoon took out a machine gun nest that was guarding the intersection of the network of roads. We left our trenches early in the morning while it was raining—the noise of the rain canceled our movement. The platoon leader split the platoon into squads and assigned each one an objective. Since my squad was the most senior, our objective was the machine gun nest. A couple of the squads were behind us, protecting our rear; three more flanked us, watching out for any counterattacks once we started advancing on the machine gun nest.

As we got closer and moved through the field, off to our right was a group of crosses. They marked some of the German dead. I made sure we moved through that area quickly. I didn't need any of my soldiers to start reflecting on their mortality.

As we got closer, I had the soldier carrying the BAR move to my right and take up an overwatch position. I told him that after we fired our rifle grenades, he was to lay down fire on the nest. The others moved with me once I saw that the BAR was in position, and we continued our movement. We were within less than one hundred feet and now waited for the artillery to commence. I looked at my watch. We had one minute till hell was about to open up in front of us.

I heard the artillery start to fire, and within seconds, the rounds impacted behind the machine gun nest. Even though they didn't see us, they started firing. Bullets were impacting in front of my position.

I ordered two of my soldiers to load rifle grenades in their rifles and fire on the nest. As the rounds started to impact, the BAR gunner fired on the nest. The nest fell silent. During the lull in firing, I got up and ran toward the nest and threw a hand grenade. Before the first one landed, I threw another. After the second, I dove onto the ground and waited. After a few minutes, I hand-signaled the soldiers to move to my position, as the BAR provided over-watch for their movement.

Once they joined me, I signaled him to move forward but remain on my flank. With still no fire from the nest, I got my squad up and moved on to the position. When we got there, we found four German soldiers with twisted and contorted legs where arms should be and arms where legs should be. The grenades were the most effective. I ordered one of my soldiers to disable the machine gun. I, along with the others, searched the dead soldiers. We took a position farther up from the nest and waited for the rest of the platoon."

JUNE 16TH, 1918

"Happy Birthday. I missed another one. I hope it's a great day. I'm still only getting one meal daily, and it's not much. Trench life gets worse every day. It seems that a lot of my soldiers are having stomach issues. So far, I'm good.

The Germans decided to shell us last night. I heard there was a direct hit on one of the trenches to our front, and there were a lot of casualties. We aren't allowed to use water for washing; it is only for drinking. It's getting unsanitary, but it is an excellent environment for rats. They are everywhere. By the looks of them, they are getting enough to eat. Maybe we should send a raiding party and follow them to where they are keeping their food. So far, I haven't wanted to eat one, and I hope the day never comes."

JUNE 21ST, 1918

"It's the first day of summer. I went on patrol earlier today, and we came across a field of red poppies. My god, it was beautiful. For a brief time, I wasn't fighting in a war but a young man walking with his girl in a lovely field, almost as beautiful as the girl holding my hand.

With the flowers, there is now green grass in the fields, and our once-starving horses, used to pull the artillery, food, and ammo, to name a few, are now enjoying every blade. They are fit and healthy again.

The skies have been clear and filled with stars for the last few nights, very much like when I sailed to France those many nights ago. I saw a shooting star the other night. I closed my eyes and made a wish. If I say the wish, it won't come true, so I will take it to my grave unless it happens before that time.

My daydreaming didn't last long. It never does. In the distance, I could hear artillery. We walked through a little village that was all but abandoned. The streets were littered with bricks from the once beautiful buildings. I thought, could or would this once quaint village ever be rebuilt? As we continued through the village, a young French girl came out of her house, or what was left of it. Chunks of brick and plaster were gone from machine gun fire or artillery blasts. I felt so sorry for her. What has this young girl done to deserve this? Oh, I forgot to say. The other day, we finally started to get more rations. We are now eating almost two meals a day. Believe it or not, just that little bit of food improved morale 100%.

As the little girl waved at us, I pulled out a can of meat and handed it to her. Her eyes lit up, and I smiled at her. She smiled back, but somehow, she knew my smile was genuine. By the look on her face, I think she could tell. In broken English, she thanked me and ran back into her house. I hope she makes it through the war. It had been a while since I smiled at something other than killing the enemy."

Alex walked out of the bathroom, looked toward his dad, and said, "I wish I had been taught more about World War I. I'm not even sure they mentioned it in school. It was brutal."

"Yes, it was like every other war fought before and after. But World War I was different. It was the first war fought with modern weapons: the machine gun, accurate artillery, gas, and airplanes, to name a few."

"Hmm, Dad, I never thought of that."

"Son, are you ready? I want to hit the road. Let's go to Soissons instead of *Compiègne*. We can go there the day before we leave. Today, we have a full day of discovery ahead of us."

"Dad sounds good, and I was born ready."

Walter walked over to Alex and hugged him. "Yep, you're my son. There is no mistaking that hell; look in the mirror."

They exited the hotel room with the diary under Alex's arm.

CHAPTER 14

SUMMER IS FOR FIGHTING

As they drove to Soissons, Alex looked out the passenger window and thought about how different everything must have looked in 1918. It was hard for him to imagine the carnage inflicted on both sides of the war, both in human and monetary terms. Reading the diary transported him to a world he had never known existed. When he got home, he wanted to learn more about the war.

His father glanced over at him. "Hey, what are you thinking about? You look in deep thought."

"Well, I haven't read any indication of why we were in World War I. It seemed to be a European issue. The Germans never attacked U.S. soil."

"Hmm, they may not have attacked the U.S., but they attacked some of our ships. I'm talking about non-military ships, like passenger and cargo ships. Not only did they attack U.S. ships, but in May 1915, they sank a British ship named the Lusitania, killing over one hundred and twenty U.S. citizens. That was two years before we declared war on Germany on April 6th, 1917."

"But what provoked the war in the first place?"

"Now, that's a complicated question. The actual war started on July 28th, 1914, when Austria-Hungary declared war on Serbia, a month after Franz Ferdinand, archduke of Austria, was assassinated while he and his wife were in Sarajevo, Bosnia and Herzegovina. Now, you want to know what's crazy? Earlier in the day, a would-be assassin threw a hand grenade into the archduke's motorcade but missed. It landed in the back of them, injuring some of his security detail. Shaken by the event, the couple decided to go to the hospital to check on one of their security guards. Their driver took a wrong turn, and while trying to turn around, a young nineteen-year-old Bosnian, Gavrilo Princip, saw the royal couple heading toward him. He moved out of the crowd and shot both Franz and Sophie. She died en route to the hospital, and he died shortly after."

"What happened to the first guy who tried to kill them?"

"Nedeljko Čabrinović escaped, took some poison, and jumped into the Miljacka River."

"The assassination started the war?"

"There's more to it, but I'm sure the assassination was what broke the camel's back."

"Earlier, you said the Germans killed over 120 Americans on the Lusitania. Why did we declare war then?"

"I don't think there was much appetite for the U.S. getting involved in a war in Europe. It was far from the U.S. borders, and the president, Woodrow Wilson, and his party at the time were more isolationist and didn't want to enter the war. I think he also believed the war would trample on individual liberties. He was worried about getting into the war because it would slow or stop his progressive reforms to the country.

"I think we finally decided to enter the war after the sinking of the Lusitania. The Germans resumed unrestricted submarine warfare. They could and would sink any ship, whether military or civilian, which happened in February 1917. Shortly after that, we severed diplomatic relations with Germany, and on April 6th, the U.S. declared war on Germany, and within three months, the first troops landed in France."

"Was the U.S. ready for war in 1917?"

"No, not really. If I remember correctly, there were approximately 125,000 soldiers in the Army, with no divisions. Hell, the Russians had the largest military before the war. The 1st Expeditionary Division was created after the U.S. declared war. It comprised units along the U.S.-Mexican border and other posts in the U.S. It consisted of infantry brigades and regiments, as well as engineering, signal, trench mortar, and artillery units. It even had an air squadron and a full divisional train. These were the first troops to land in France in June 1917. It was later changed to the 1st Infantry Division, which, by the way, still exists and has fought in almost every major conflict or war the U.S. has been involved in since. The only one it didn't fight in was the Korean War, since it was positioned in Europe after the Second World War in case the Soviets invaded Europe."

"Damn, Dad, you sure know a lot about the war."

"Well, when you started to read the diary, I decided to learn more about the war. I didn't know much before we started this adventure, mainly what I saw in movies like Sergeant York and some documentaries. I did read one fascinating article dated January 1917. Germany offered portions of the United States to Mexico if they would join the Central Powers."

"What, now that is crazy. What did they offer?"

"Well, for one, where we live, Texas. The others were New Mexico and Arizona. Heck, Arizona and New Mexico just became states in 1912. The Germans sought to return to Mexico what they considered its lost territories. My thinking is that if they got the Mexicans involved, we wouldn't be able to commit a large number of troops to fight in Europe. It would open a southern front in the U.S."

"Wow, that would have made a huge difference in Europe. The Germans might have won."

"Yep, that it would. The Army was not ready to fight a war in Europe and, most of all, a trench war. Even though the first troops arrived in June 1917, France and Britain knew it would take months for the Army to be ready for combat and have an impact on the war. Remember, in his diary, he wrote about all the training and who was doing the training. But all the training paid off when the Army got into the fight."

"Surely the U.S. put more than 125,000 troops in Europe to fight?"

"Many more, Alex. Over four million men had served in the Army, with an additional 800,000 in the other branches. Now, not all of those four million or so volunteered. In 1917, Congress passed the Selective Service Act, commonly known as the draft today. Around 500,000 were drafted, fewer than the number the government had hoped for. By the summer of 1918, over two million soldiers were in Europe, and not all were on the front."

"So, Dad, how did they drive recruitment?

"Have you ever seen one of the 'Uncle Sam Wants You' posters?"

"Yes, of course. The recruiter brought one to school."

"Well, that is all it took, a little bit of marketing."

"Interesting. So, based on his writings, our unknown soldier was among the first to arrive in Europe."

"Yep, I would say so. And that's all I know about World War I for now. Let's get some lunch before we arrive."

"Sounds good. I'm starving. Thanks for the quick history lesson."

Alex opened the diary and started reading.

June 27th, 1918

"I'm still back in the rear area but staying busy. I got a new soldier in my squad. He is from Ohio and is eager to get into the fight. I remember those days. I'm not as enthusiastic as I once was. The weather has been great, with very little rain, but the trenches we are drilling in remain muddy. Today, I took the squad and their gear to the delousing tent to eliminate everything, including lice and any other pests we had been exposed to in the trenches. Then, off to a bath. What being clean does to one is fantastic.

We played baseball today. Wow, it's been a while since I last played. It's an excellent way for the guys to relieve stress and get some physical activity without the day-to-day exercise and drills we do. A couple of the guys started hitting the bottle, and I'm doing everything possible to keep them busy. I talked to one of them, and he told me he had never drunk liquor before the war. Now, it is his only way to relax. I offered to take him to the Chaplain. He declined, and I needed to keep him busy. By the way, we lost the baseball game."

July 5th, 1918

"Another 4th of July in France, it seems so long ago. Some of the soldiers I marched with in Paris last year are no longer with us. Everything in the area was spotless, and there was a lot of competition among the units. Each infantry platoon in the brigade was assigned tasks to complete in a specific timeframe. Once they were completed, they were judged by the staff officers. One of the competitions was to design the best camouflage for an observation post. The sound of airplanes could be heard in the middle of the competition. Not knowing if they were friendly or enemy, everyone stopped and took defensive positions. It didn't take long until they were identified as friendly and returned to camouflaging their OPs.

Another competition my platoon participated in was marching—excuse me, the Army calls it drilling. We did pretty well. We didn't win, but we looked good.

To close out the night, the artillery batteries fired what sounded like hundreds, if not thousands, of rounds toward the Germans. I heard the shells contained mustard gas that the French gave us.

After all the day's activities, I returned to my bunk and thought about the last 4th of July we spent together. It was sure hot, but it was a little cooler under that big oak. The picnic basket you put together was great. I was so full as we lay on the blanket, eating bread and cheese and drinking red wine. A band played in the background, and the wind blew through your hair. I would brush it to the side, and you would say, 'I hate long hair. I'm going to get it cut just like yours.' I replied, 'Please no, I love it long." It was like we had the whole park to ourselves, even though it was packed with families. I miss you. We must have waited four or five hours for the fireworks.

The only fireworks we had today were from the artillery. But that night, they were beautiful, and they seemed like they lasted forever. The massive red, white, and blue display was terrific. The sounds and the lit-up sky seem so long ago. Now, when I see the sky light up and hear the sounds, I duck down and wait for the impact of shells and the death that will follow. I pray I can go to a fireworks display without sweating and anxiety. I will need you next to me."

July 7th, 1918

"The training has gotten more intense. Something is afoot. The training schedule for the next couple of weeks is as if we were in combat. We will be living in the trenches during that time. For those of us who have lived in them before, this is nothing new; however, it will be a rude awakening for the new ones. I'm going to keep my eyes on the new guy from Ohio. I heard the Germans were on the offensive from the area we were just in before we were relieved. It's been so hot that they issued us some tan shorts. I hate wearing them. They look so unprofessional. The bugs and everything else in the trenches will feast on our legs."

As they pulled into the parking lot, Alex closed the diary.

CHAPTER 15

BACK TO THE FRONT

VILLERS-COTTERÊTS, FRANCE

With only a few more miles to travel, Walter decided to stop for lunch in the town of Villers-Cotterêts.

"Dad, why are we stopping? Aren't we headed to Soissons?"

"We are. I thought I would stop here first. This town saw some of the worst fighting of the war. When the war started, the castle was turned into a hospital." He pointed to his right.

They exited the car to explore the town. It was a cloudy day that looked like it was about to rain. Alex saw a lovely little café to his right. "Dad, do you want to get something to eat before we continue to Soissons?"

Walter nodded. "I could use a coffee and maybe a pastry."

They walked in and found a table in the back, facing the busy city center. Even with the impending rain, the city center was full of shoppers.

The waitress came to the table and took their orders. Alex got a Coke and some fries, and Walter got a coffee and a profiterole—a light pastry filled with cream.

As they waited for their order, Alex said, "Dad, thank you again for asking me on this vacation. It has been more than I could have ever imagined. Before we left, my friends told me that I would only visit Paris, the museums, and the wine country, and hang out. I was expecting a boring time. They said I should have asked you to go to Hawaii. At least there would have been girls." He laughed as the waitress arrived with their order.

Alex picked up his Coke. "Well, this has been anything but boring. This has been the most exciting and best vacation I've ever been on. I've learned so much about World War I through the eyes of an unknown soldier, but most of all, I learned a lot about myself."

"What do you mean?"

"I didn't know I could be so passionate about history. This soldier's diary has opened my eyes to a new world, where the past shapes the present. I feel compassion for the soldier, even though I never knew him. His family must have been devastated to learn of his death. I wonder if they ever got his body and were able to bury him."

"That's a good question. So far, from what we have read, it's tough to determine even what unit he was in without some digging. However, I know that the First Expeditionary Division was the first unit deployed to France. So far, he hasn't given anyone's name, first or last. But as we continue to read, maybe there will be a clue."

"Yep, we will have to see. Based on his writings, I continue to have dreams about him, but I can never see his face. I can see everyone else's but not his."

"Maybe he wants to remain unknown."

"Dad, do we have time to read more before exploring the city?"

"Sure, it's nice relaxing here with you. Maybe, just maybe, the weather will clear."

Alex started to read from the diary.

July 11th, 1918

"Well, we got our orders to prepare to move to the front. I need to get the

guys back in the fight. There is so much drinking, gambling, and whoring in the rear. I heard the fighting up there has been most brutal, if there is even such a thing. I'm getting my squad ready and checking everyone's equipment. I'm ensuring they have their identification disks on, just in case. Their lives are in my hands. The new guy from Ohio is learning very quickly, but I will still keep an eye on him. We are being loaded onto trucks tomorrow to get us to the front quickly. At least we will be rested from not having to march all the way."

JULY 12TH, 1918

"I would have rather marched up to the front. The ride in the truck was terrible. The roads weren't smooth. There were holes every twenty feet or so. We bounced all over the place and were jammed in like sardines. A couple of the guys got sick, and I felt like it, but I couldn't show weakness to my men. Not with us going to the front. I just closed my eyes and thought of you. It calmed me down. I'm rethinking being in the sidecar on the motorcycle. Heck, maybe I should volunteer to fly.

We got behind the front lines early this morning and are about to move into the trenches. The men's faces said a thousand words without a single word being spoken. This seems different and hard to explain. As we got out of the trucks, there were hundreds of German soldiers who were captured and moving to the rear. Every one of them I saw was wounded. The ones who were blinded by gas held onto the shirt of the one in front of them. I counted at least fifty of them. Gas is such an evil way to fight. I'm glad the wind was blowing away from us. I didn't have the energy to put on my gas mask. The only way I get back in one of those trucks is to go home, sitting or lying flat."

JULY 14TH, 1918

"Infantrymen like to walk and walk again as we did last night. I must say, in the trucks, I felt so vulnerable. At least when we are walking, we can fight and protect ourselves, and we did. The Germans launched an air raid on us once we got into position. Not only were they strafing us, but they were also dropping bombs from their airplanes. The bombs weren't very effective,

but they play with your mind. You can hear them whistle as they descend to the ground. Now, to make things even worse, it started to rain, and given the air attacks, we couldn't make any fires to cook our food. I'm starving, wet, and muddy—a great day to be a soldier. Looking back at it, maybe it was good that it started to rain and cloud over. The German planes couldn't see through the clouds, and if they got too low to the ground, our machine guns opened up on them. Watching the tracer rounds from the German planes and our machine guns was mesmerizing. They found that out quickly. Our gunners could shoot one of them down, and that was so close to the ground that I could see him waving. Then I watched it as it flew into the woods and exploded.

Once the air raids were over, I went to each squad member to check on them. They were all in good spirits, considering they were as hungry, wet, and muddy- basically miserable- as I was. However, I didn't let them know. The weather has been pitiful and muddy, even in the woods, where we await orders. They, along with me, are eager to get into the fight. I wanted to check on my soldier who was wounded the other day. So, before we left, I went to the medical tent and checked on him before they moved him. He is doing good but lost his leg and is being transported back to a hospital, then off to the U.S. He said they were going to put him in an ambulance. The ambulance drivers are excellent, and the Red Cross makes a great target on top of the wagons. We did get a replacement for him, so the squad is at full strength.

I'm a little worried about the young man from Ohio; he is starting to alienate himself. I can't have that happen. He will be sticking with me."

July 15th, 1918

"We relieved a Moroccan unit last night. That was tricky. We sent out an advanced patrol to make contact. Once contact was established, we started moving into the trenches. It was pitch black outside; I couldn't distinguish what was before me. We relieved them without any incidents. The trench was in good shape, and I placed my squad in their positions and waited for the word to attack. When daylight came, I could see what we would encounter. We were all beat, but sleep was not a thing we could do right now as the squad was getting familiar with the battlefield. I got word to take three

soldiers from my squad and assist the field artillery guys with locating a forward observation post and securing it till they returned with their forward observers. I took Ohio and one other soldier. We walked down to a point in the trench and waited for the artillery soldiers. It didn't take long for them to show up. I asked the lieutenant if he had already picked out a spot. He took out a map and showed it to me. It was a little depression about three hundred yards in front of us. I told him we would go over the wire first and bring his team over if we didn't encounter any enemy fire. I won't ever forget the look on his face. I could tell he had not been over the trench yet. It wasn't a look of fright, more of determination. I told him my name, and he told me his name, 'Harry Truman.' He seemed like a nice guy with a mid-west accent."

"Alex, stop for a second. Does the name Harry Truman ring a bell?"

"Do you think he met a future president?"

"Well, I know that President Truman was an artillery officer in the war."

"Dang, that's so cool. Just think: If he had let him go over the trench first, he could have been killed and changed the course of the 20th century."

"Keep reading."

"He patted me on the shoulder and said, 'Let's get to it, Corporal.' I looked at my men and nodded. With that, Ohio put his foot on the ladder and went over. I followed, and behind me was the other soldier. Once we got out a few yards, I waved the lieutenant over with his men. As we got closer, we were spotted. German machine guns opened up on us. We all hit the ground. I looked around, and everyone was in one piece. I went over to where the lieutenant was lying on the ground, prone. He stuck his head up, and I pushed it down as the German machine gun opened up—bullets missed him by inches. He looked at me and said, 'Thank you, Corporal.'"

"Dad, holy cow, he saved a future president's life."

"I would have said something else, but holy cow is good. But damn."

"Ohio had the BAR, and he opened up on the Germans. Keeping low, I moved to the flank of the machine gun. It was too far for a hand grenade, but it was between us and where we needed to put the OP. I took my flare gun out of its holster, put in a red flare, and fired it. Within a few minutes, artillery shells began raining down on the German machine gun positions. After the initial shelling, the machine gun fell silent. I motioned for my patrol to move forward. We reached the depression, and the lieutenant set up his observation post. I sent one man back to let them know we had secured the area and were waiting to be relieved. It was getting dark by the time we were relieved. I bid the lieutenant farewell. My two other soldiers and I returned to the trench right before a downpour. It didn't take long for the trench to fill up with water. I debriefed my company commander, returned to my position, and awaited orders."

JULY 17TH, 1918

"Last night, we moved into another position. It was the darkest night I had ever seen. The infantry moved in columns along the road. Typically, we have a reasonable distance between soldiers, but last night, we had to put one arm on the shoulder of the soldier in front of us. After a couple of hours, we made it to our new wood line. Food has been a hit or miss. As the sun rose, a runner told me that a soup kitchen had been set up down the road and that I could filter my squad through to get something to eat. I let all my soldiers go first, and then I followed. I must say, it was pretty damn good. Now, it's not as good as yours, though.

We set up our positions in the woods and waited for the orders to move. Off to our right are the French tanks, some in position, others moving down the road. The roar of the engines was a comforting sound, but deafening. They will support us when we attack in the open fields. They are not used in the forest. There is no way they can maneuver. They would be sitting ducks. The French planes will provide aerial reconnaissance. The Germans are dug in and are well-positioned to defend against our attack. There is a marsh to our left. I was told to tell my men not to go in it. It was contaminated with yperite from the heavy German shelling, and it was causing burns on some of the soldiers who came in contact with the water. I hope it rains to mask our sound and movement in the open. Either way, I'm going to pray. The Germans are dug in and waiting for us to attack. I'm double-checking on my men. I told them to switch off and try to get some sleep."

CHAPTER 16

SIX DAYS IN HELL

CAFÉ: VILLERS-COTTERÊTS, FRANCE

As they sat in the café waiting for the weather to change, Alex continued to read from the diary, engrossed in the author's writings. His writing seemed to come alive as he wrote about the war. Having not seen combat, he couldn't fathom what his dad had seen and done.

He looked over at his dad. "You know you have always been my hero."

His dad glanced over and smiled. The joy in his heart was not measurable. He replied, "I only want to be your dad."

July 18th, 1918 – Day 1

"We bivouacked close to where the attack will begin. The terrain is rolling hills and waist-high yellow wheat fields. It would be a beautiful place if it were not for the war. What's missing are the trenches. I'm unsure if that is a good thing. We have to find cover where we can, and where there is none, we dig.

The orders came down at 4:25 a.m. Artillery would pummel the No-man's-land in front of our positions. I looked at my watch. It would start at

4:30 a.m. My hand was shaking again; it was not nerves. I think it was excitement. I looked at Ohio, who was next to me, and said, 'Five minutes, pass it down.'

I counted down the minutes: 4 minutes, 3 minutes, 2 minutes, and 1 minute, and at precisely 4:30 a.m., the artillery began its bombardment of the enemy's defensive positions. When the barrage began, my squad and the rest of the battalion got up and ran toward the enemy. We all screamed like uncaged animals. My adrenaline flowed, I heard my heartbeat in my ears, and my legs felt weak, but I was almost running. Only the light from the shelling impact provided any light on this very dark night. As I advanced, I ensured my squad stayed in line with the rest of the platoon. I looked to my left and heard a now-familiar sound. The sound of French tanks showed that they had taken up positions between the platoon and were firing their machine guns with deadly accuracy.

As we got closer, the German machine guns opened up. Not one soldier stopped or slowed down. We all continued to move forward. I looked off to my right and could see the platoon leader. He had his pistol out, leading his men. I felt proud to be part of this platoon as I glanced at him again. He fell to the ground. The machine gun fire found a victim. I didn't stop. I continued to move and keep my squad fighting. I was almost out of breath when I heard my soldier from Bald Knob scream. I looked to my right, and he was down. I moved to where he was, and he lay there in a pool of water that was turning red with his blood. I felt dizzy. There was nothing I could do for him. I put my hand in his shirt, pulled one of the identification tags, and put it in my pocket. Bullets flew by my head. I felt the sting of a bullet as it grazed my arm. I heard in my mind, 'Get up and move. You have a squad to lead. Get up, Get up.'

I got back up and looked down the line at my squad. We were continuing to move. As we progressed, the artillery would shift their shelling, ensuring they weren't hitting friendly soldiers. The artillery's accuracy was amazing. At that time, I thought back to the artillery lieutenant, Harry Truman.

The sun started to rise, and I heard and saw French airplanes over the battlefield. One got so close that a fragment from a shell took him down. He managed to turn his plane around and crash behind our lines. I looked in the direction he came from, and I could see more planes approaching in the distance. When they got over our heads, they fired their machine guns.

We made it to our first objective by 5:30 a.m. Our artillery had been very effective as we entered the German defenses. However, there was still some resistance. We killed as many as we could, and the rest surrendered. Even with our fellow soldiers falling all around us and the German machine gun fire, we were undaunted. Not only were we fighting the Germans, but we were fighting fatigue and forgot all about the danger we were in and that death waited at every footstep we took.

By the time we got to objective one, the only one I had lost was the soldier from Bald Knob. I'm going to miss him. He started to write letters to his family. He was so proud of himself, and I was proud of him. Learning how to read and write in almost daily combat is some accomplishment. When he wrote his first letter home, the look in his eyes was worth every second I spent with him. I crawled along the line to check on my soldiers. A couple of them had minor wounds, but they were all in the fight.

We had twenty minutes to check our gear and get ready to advance to the next objective. Two minutes before we moved on to our next objective, I yelled, 'Two minutes.' At precisely twenty minutes after getting to our first objective, I heard the whistle to move out. We got up without hesitation. Like earlier, we were ready to fight. We were a fierce fighting force after months of combat, living in the trenches and fighting in No man's land. We are the infantry!

The ground favored the enemy, allowing them to place their deadly machine guns effectively. As we advanced, we started to take heavy casualties. The ground was so uneven as I ran. I would run into a crater, exit it, and then enter another. There was no end to the craters. It was like running on a wooden footbridge. As I ran, I would shoot my rifle, not aiming but putting it waist high and pulling the trigger. Ohio, with the BAR, was firing at a steady rate. Screams filled the battlefield as soldiers started to fall.

Once we reached our second objective, we had forty minutes to regroup and prepare for the next objective. I looked back to where we had just run through, and I could already see the stretcher-bearers treating the wounded even as the Germans shelled the area and machine gun fire raked the area. These were some brave soldiers. They didn't even carry weapons. They would run through a hail of bullets to get to a soldier, hoping to save his life. Once they had stabilized the soldier to the point where he could be moved, they would place him on a litter, and a couple of soldiers would escort him back to either a medical tent or an ambulance. As I watched them, I thought, 'Damn, the war would be over if everyone were just wounded. When a soldier is killed, it's just him, but when a soldier is wounded, it's at least two to three soldiers off the battlefield.'

The next objective was beyond a deep ravine, over a half-mile wide. In the middle of the ravine was a swamp at least six hundred yards wide with a deep stream running through the swamp. The side of the ravine was steep, and it was a challenge to go down and climb out of the ravine. The Germans had dug into the ravine and had gun emplacements in every key location. On the high ground, the Germans turned the ravine into a giant killing field. We sustained a large number of casualties. My squad was no different. We lost two more in the battle. One was a new guy who had joined the platoon only five days ago—tragic.

When we climbed down the western side of the ravine and made it about three hundred yards to the east, the Germans opened up with heavy machine guns and direct fire from artillery. This was the first time we encountered direct fire from artillery. It was devastating.

We fought our way through the terrain and maneuvered through the area as the machine gun and artillery shells impacted all around us. We were close enough for them to fire directly at us, but they were out of range from our rifles. We had to get closer. The tanks that were with us were now worthless. The Germans took all of them out. The counter-battery fire was not effective. The terrain of the ravine favored the Germans.

I jumped into a crater next to me, and in another crater was Ohio with the BAR. To my right was what was left of my squad. No more than one hundred feet to our left was a German machine gun nest. They had not detected us and were firing to their front. I motioned for everyone to stay down. I took a grenade from my belt and crawled toward the machine gun nest. Still undetected, I poked my head up to check the distance between me and the nest. I could see I still had around fifty feet left. I put my head down and crawled for another few feet. I looked up, pulled the pin, released the spoon, counted to five, got on one knee, tossed the grenade, and got back down. After a couple of seconds, boom, the machine gun nest fell silent.

I then ordered my squad up to my location. As they crawled to my location, I turned and lay on my back, breathing so hard I thought my chest would rip apart. My hands were shaking again. When my squad was in position, I motioned for them to move out. I got up first and covered Ohio as he moved. As I moved, Ohio covered me as I advanced up the side of the ravine. When I got to the bottom of the embankment, I motioned for Ohio to move up while the other members covered his move. Machine guns were blazing. I concentrated my efforts in front of me and covered Ohio as he moved into position.

I felt movement next to me and looked over. There was Ohio, bleeding from machine gun fire. He just looked at me and smiled. I could see in his eyes that time was running out for him. His skin had turned a gray color against the dark mud of the ravine. I took out his dressing and applied pressure to his wounds. As I did that, the rest of the squad moved to my position. One of the other soldiers helped me attempt to stop the bleeding. There was no use. He died in my arms. I handed his BAR to the other soldier and said, 'Come on, let's move out.' Before I left Ohio alone in the ravine in France on a hot summer day, I put one of his identification tags in my pocket. I'm going to miss him. He was a good soldier. I have another letter to write. Every day, it gets more challenging to fathom all the deaths.

Our artillery finally found its target and removed most of the German machine gun nests and their artillery. No more direct fire. Damn, that was pure evil. When a round hit a soldier, there was nothing left. I have no idea how we can identify them.

By the afternoon, the German commander had surrendered, with most of his men dead. He decided to spare the rest of his soldiers. We took a lot of prisoners. We were told to hold the line till another infantry unit supplemented us. I turned to talk to Ohio, but he wasn't there anymore. I'm exhausted, and so are the rest of my men, what's left of them. I feel like I have failed them."

"Damn, Dad, he lost two of his most trusted men."

"He will have to start trusting some new ones. I'm more worried about him feeling like a bad leader. It will be interesting to see how he gets out of his slump."

"Do you think he's a good leader?"

"I do. He didn't cause any of their deaths by mistakes or bad decisions. Hell, go back and read. He always takes the lead. He has every trait of a good leader."

"What traits?"

"There are eighteen traits. The ones that stick out to me are communication, knowing and caring for his men, courage, loyalty, leading, training your soldiers as a team, and setting an example. The only one I'm worried about is confidence."

"So, how does he regain it?"

"He has to get back in the fight; he has to."

Alex continued to read out of the diary.

"Today was bloody and costly for everyone on both sides of the war. As night fell, the atmosphere was mostly quiet, with only the occasional sound of artillery. I received three new soldiers in my platoon to replace the losses we had. I introduced them to the squad and explained their responsibilities. I assigned one of them to Ohio's BAR. I need to assign guard duty for tonight. I will take the last shift so that I'm ready for the battle that is on the horizon. It's time to try to get some rest. Tomorrow will be another bloody day. As I sat down, the sun hit my jacket, and I saw the reflection of Ohio's blood on it. I don't know if I'm sad, mad, guilt-ridden, or emotionless. It was the worst day so far. My uniform looks nothing like it did in June, those many days ago."

JULY 19TH, 1918 – DAY 2

"It's early, a little before 1:00 a.m., while I was on watch. The platoon runner told me I was needed at the company command post. I woke another soldier to continue my watch. I gathered my gear and ran to the post. The CO gave the order of the operations once everyone was gathered. The attack would start at 4:00 a.m. Our mission was to provide security for the left

flank and provide reconnaissance patrols. By the time he told us who would do the reconnaissance patrols, I raised my hand and volunteered my squad."

"Son, it looks like he still has confidence in his ability to lead."

"He nodded and said, 'Okay, Corporal, your squad is a go. See me after the briefing so I can give out your orders.' I sat there after volunteering. I thought the soldiers I lost yesterday would have wanted to do the mission. The CO finished his briefing and told me to stand by. As I waited, I walked over to the battle map and some photos from our reconnaissance airplanes. I could see the Germans had multiple tiers of defense, the most formidable being machine guns. 'They have quit the defense setup, Corporal.' Yes, sir, they do. The number of machine gun nests is the most I have ever seen in one location. 'Yes, there are a lot of them. Your mission is to scout their flank. We don't have good intelligence if there is a gap between these two units,' the CO said as he pointed to the map. We haven't been able to get any new photos or drawings since yesterday.'

We reviewed the map, and they gave me my final instructions: 'Your recon patrol leaves in forty-five minutes. You have a six-minute time frame to cross the LD. I need to know if there is a gap by 3:30 a.m.. I exited the CP and ran back to my squad. When I got back, I told the soldier on guard to wake the rest and meet me at my location in ten minutes.

Everyone was there within ten minutes, even the new guys. This will be their first recon patrol and first time in combat. I went over the mission with them and told them to be ready to move in five minutes. My hands started shaking again. Sweat rolled down my face. I wiped it off and continued to prep for my mission. I verified I had a red and green flare. The red flare was used if there was no gap between units, and the green flare was used if there was. The squad was assembled and ready to go as I finished my prep.

We went to where we would move to the LD. I looked at my watch, and we had ten minutes to make the exit point. I told the team to keep down, and off we went into the dark abyss of no man's land—ninety minutes to complete my mission.

We got to the point where we crossed the LD right on time. The silence was eerie. We moved quietly but with a purpose in a single column. I was in the middle, and one of my senior squad members was leading and navigating to the location. The new soldiers were behind me. Suddenly, the point man stopped and gave the hand signal to get down. We all lay flat on the ground. I crawled up to him and whispered, 'What's going on?'

'Corporal, there is a sentry post manned by two. I see a way around, but it'll add a few minutes.' I didn't give it a second thought. 'Go around.' I let him move out. He veered off to his right, and we followed undetected. As we continued to advance, German artillery started firing. Shells landed on the troops on the line. The sound of the artillery would mask any noise we made, and we had some time to make up. I walked quickly toward my point man and told him we needed to move faster as long as there was artillery fire. He moved out with some pep in his step, but still moved without being detected.

I could see we were within a couple of minutes of our target. I looked at my watch. We had five minutes to go. I gathered the squad and put out two soldiers. One to watch the left, the other to watch the right. The point man, another soldier, and I moved toward the objective. Once we were on the objective, I could see a small gap between the machine gun nest. Someone didn't do a very good job laying wire. However, I didn't think the gap was large enough to be exploited by our forces. We moved back to where the other soldiers were. I looked at my watch: 3:00 a.m. I removed the flare gun, inserted a red flare, pointed it at the sky, and pulled the trigger. The sky lit up red, and at the same time, the flare exploded in the air. German machine guns opened up with a fury, unlike anything I had ever seen. A wall of green tracers buzzed over our heads, and all we could hear was the rat-rat-rat-tat of the guns, almost like a buzzing sound. We got as low as we could. They were firing widely, but we hadn't been detected. I then decided that, given the sheer volume of fire, we would stay put and wait for the attack to begin in about twenty minutes.

To our rear, we could hear and see the attack coming our way. My only hope was that the unit advancing toward us knew we were there. I prayed they did. The machine gun fire was unabated on the advancing infantry. I knew we had to do something. I couldn't let my fellow soldiers get mowed down. The nearest machine gun nest was fifty yards to our left. I motioned for the squad to follow me. As we started to move, an infantry platoon advanced to our location. The lieutenant yelled, 'Green for go, Red for no go.' I replied, 'Red.'

He moved next to me after giving orders to his platoon sergeant to create a line to my left and right. I could see his platoon had taken heavy casualties. The lieutenant noticed a gap to our left and told me to stay there. He would take what was left of his platoon to attack the strong point, wreaking havoc on the soldiers. I informed him that my squad would accompany him since our mission was complete. As we began to move up the hilltop, we encountered some French soldiers, and after a bit of convincing from the lieutenant, they decided to join us. The lieutenant was a born leader. He guided us through machine gun fire and rifle fire. When we got to the crest of the hill, he then led us toward the enemy, running through the hail of bullets. We continued as the bullets flew past our heads, landing next to us and even finding their targets. We were on pure adrenaline, and the leadership of the lieutenant was unlike anything I had ever witnessed. The shock to the Germans of a bunch of American and French soldiers running toward them threw them off balance. This daring move allowed us to capture six machine guns and forty prisoners. With those six machine guns out of action, the rest of the unit advanced and joined with another, but the fighting wasn't over yet.

I made my way to the lieutenant, noticing his foot bleeding. I offered to treat the wound, but he declined. I could see he was in much pain, but he continued to lead his unit. I could see my unit to my right and said, 'Lieutenant ...' He answered, 'It's Parker. Yes, Corporal.'

'Lieutenant Parker, my unit is over there. I'm going to take my squad and rejoin them. Sir, you're a brave man.'

He replied, 'Roger, Corporal, you're one brave man, too.'

I rejoined my platoon and continued the fight and attack. At 5:30 p.m., we were ordered to launch another attack. The goal was to finish before dark, allowing us to dig in and conceal our positions so that enemy artillery couldn't see us. I'm sitting in my foxhole writing, not the most comfortable, but at least I'm not in a damn trench."

July 20th, 1918 – Day 3

"We got a late start today. The artillery didn't start till noon. Not that we got to sleep in, but we were all ready throughout the night. The Germans want the ground we took from them. At 2:00 p.m., another bout of heavy shelling from our artillery was landing in front of our lines, prepping the battlefield for our movement. The first unit that went over the knoll in front of us met a wall of bullets and a heavy round of shelling. I could see the dead and wounded. They were decimated, and we were following. We moved in a column formation along the outer perimeter of the ravine. We were spaced at least fifteen feet apart. As we continued to move, I heard the familiar whistle that signaled a halt to movement. We all stopped, got down, and waited for the whistle to move. As I lay on the ground, I thought of you. I want to see you one more time, just one. The whistle to move brought me back to reality. I got up and motioned for my squad to follow me.

We started across a large open area, and as we were crossing, something unusual happened, or, should I say, didn't happen. We crossed the open area without any German machine gun fire or artillery shelling. It was like a walk in the park, a deadly park.

Off in the distance, I heard the sound of artillery shells. The rounds were impacting in what seemed like one continuous boom. I could imagine the effects it had on the soldiers. If you got hit by one of the shells, it would be like the soldier disappeared. Others, not killed, would be totally confused and wander aimlessly until machine gun fire kills them.

In the afternoon, we made it to our objective with almost the same number of soldiers. This was a good day."

July 21st, 1918 – Day 4

"Another attack today, and the dead and wounded are in proportions I could have never imagined. The dead litter the battlefield, draped over the wire, upright in shell craters, and lying in the open fields. We have to combine units to muster enough soldiers to mount the attacks. Everyone was fatigued and hungry, but we had courage. The men who make up this unit are a fighting force never seen before, and I'm proud to be a part of it.

My squad was attached to another infantry platoon, and we were posi-

tioned on the left flank and waited for the order to move. At 4:45 a.m., without artillery support, we went on the attack. In front of us were the steep ridges, thick brush, and the deadly open fields. The Germans had the area covered by machine fire. Our only advantage was the night. Before we mounted our attack, I ensured the squad was ready, bayonets fixed, and gas masks prepped. It was going to be another hot summer day in France, trying to stay alive for the next attack. It seems like a never-ending cycle.

As we moved within the ravine, the sun started to come up. There was not a cloud in the sky. What you notice when there is calm in the fighting is amazing. We didn't have contact till we crested the ravine and were on the plateau. As the first group of soldiers exited the ravine, the machine guns opened up on them. Soldiers were stopped in their tracks by the hail of bullets and started falling back into the ravine. Ordinary men would stop, but not us. We continued moving out of the ravine but kept lower to the ground. Even with the mud, thick brush, and relentless machine gun and artillery, we held the line steady as we advanced. As I ran, I tried to imagine what the German soldiers must have thought. Have they ever seen a more determined army advancing on them, or did they think we were all insane? The bullets passing next to my head woke me up. I didn't even realize I was starting to get ahead of the unit. One of my soldiers ran over to me, grabbed me by my shoulder, and said, 'Corporal, you are going to get yourself killed. Slow down and get down!' I did just what he said, and thank god I did. Otherwise, I would've run straight into one of our artillery barrages covering our move.

Once the barrage lifted, we rallied behind our captain and captured a German artillery gun and its crew. The crew looked almost happy. They would leave the battlefield and put it behind them. Their war was over. There was no light at the end of my war tunnel. But there is no way I want to get captured."

July 22nd, 1918 – Day 5

"We haven't even had time to bury our dead and look for any wounded. We were trying to retrieve them from the battlefield by snipers wreaking havoc on the soldiers tasked to get our dead. It's not only the snipers but also the attacks from the air. The ground war here may be all but over, but no one

told the German pilots as they continued to drop bombs on us. Today, we just held the line. I had some time to write the letters to Ohio and my friend from Bald Knob. I'm getting good at writing them, damn it! I must take them to the company headquarters so the commander can review them. I have no idea when they will be mailed or if they will reach them before the Army notifies them.

I hate just sitting around. My mind starts to wander."

July 23rd, 1918 – Day 6

"Yesterday was the last day of this battle, and the units that participated looked nothing like they did before. Most of the leadership was dead or wounded. A lieutenant commanded our company; another company had a private in charge. The battalion had a captain in charge. If we had to fight again, we would, but it would have been on sheer grit. There was a void of leadership that no unit should ever have to endure. What is so painful is the loss of so many fighters. The privates, corporals, sergeants, and junior offi-cers. These are the hardest to replace. I know; I had to replace a couple. I mourn for their families."

Walter put down his coffee cup and looked outside. The once-gray sky was now bright blue. "Come on, let's get to Soissons. There is one other place I would like to visit today. We might be getting back to Paris late, but what the hell. It will be worth it."

CHAPTER 17

LISTENING POST

1ST DIVISION MONUMENT: BUZANCY, FRANCE

As they drove to Soissons, Alex said, "Dad, I still can't believe two wars were fought on this land. It looks so beautiful. Do you know much about the battle that took place here? Do you think our unknown soldier fought here?"

"Son, this land has seen so much death and destruction. I know a little about the battle, and yes, I believe he fought here. Our first stop will be the 1st Division Monument. It's right outside of town, near Buzancy."

They sat silently, pulling onto the grassy area close to the monument but off the road.

Alex was the first one out of the car, the soldier's diary still in his hands. Before Walter exited the car, he took out his phone and searched for the 1st Division Monument at Soissons. He wanted to give Alex the correct information. Both met at the front of the car and walked toward the monument. As Alex got closer, an uneasy feeling came over him. It was not a sick feeling but more of a kind of presence, sorrow. They walked up to the beautiful, tall, white marble structure surrounded by a green iron fence. On top of the structure was a beautiful hawk with its wings protecting the 1st Division patch, surrounded by a wreath.

Alex stared at the patch. "Dad, I've seen that patch before in one of your army pictures, right?"

"Yes, you sure have. I was in the 1st Infantry Division, also known as the "Big Red One."

"Dad, that is so cool."

As they got closer, Alex said, "Look at all the names. My God, did all of these men die in the battle that happened here?"

"Yes. Engraved in black marble are the names of over 2,213 division soldiers killed in the battle over just four days. Now, the number of wounded was 6,347 division soldiers. It was a very bloody and costly battle. Remember, it was one of the first large-scale battles involving soldiers, where the soldiers were under the control of U.S. generals. They fought in others before, but this was a large-scale offensive."

Alex stared at his father. "In the diary, he described six days of battle."

"Correct. The last two days were more defensive and mopped up any resistance."

Alex started reading the heroes' names when a thought struck him. "Dad, the names of Ohio and the soldier from Bald Knob are on this monument. My god, we know how and when they died."

"Alex, too bad we don't know their names. But we know they were identified. He ensured he took an identification tag from each one and left one with the bodies."

Alex noticed a section listing the names of missing soldiers in action. "Hey, Dad, did you see this section with the names of the missing in action?"

Walter walked over, stared at the names, and replied, "There are so many for so few days of battle. God rest their souls."

They spent twenty minutes at the monument. As they stood there and viewed the monument, Alex took out the diary and re-read the pages detailing the deaths of Ohio and the soldier from Bald Knob. As he read, a tear rolled down his cheek. He felt like he was crying for the unknown soldier since Alex knew he didn't cry when they were killed. He had a mission to complete, and there was no time for emotions.

While they stood there, Walter waved his arm from left to right. "In the fields from left to right and the villages, there were 125,000 casualties from the days of the attack. The U.S. had 12,000, but that's nothing compared to the French and British. France lost the majority with 95,000. While the British had 18,000."

"Hold on, did you just say the French had 95,000 casualties in just four days of fighting?"

"Yes, as crazy as that sounds."

"That's like over 31,250 combined casualties per day."

"Son, the Germans had 168,000 casualties."

Alex's mouth gaped open for a moment. "This ground has seen a lot of killing, not only in World War I but also in World War II. Dad, the unknown soldier who wrote this diary, walked these fields with his soldiers. I can almost feel him." Alex stood there and took it all in. He moved closer to his father, put his arm around him, and said, "Let's go, Soldier, but where are we going next?"

"Well, it's just down the road. You'll see when we get there. Deal?"

"Deal, and thank you again."

They walked back to their car. Alex turned around, saluted, and whispered, "Who are you? You may be unknown, but you're not forgotten."

Once in the car, Alex asked, "How long is the ride to our next destination?"

"Around twenty or thirty minutes, depending on traffic. Why?"

As Alex grabbed the diary, he replied, "I'm going to read a little bit."

July 26th, 1918

"Yesterday was great. The weather was fantastic, and the sun warmed my

soul. The entire unit was able to gather. Each battalion had a marshaling area where we assembled. Once we got there, hot food was waiting for us. My God, it was so good. The cooks went out of their way to ensure we had enough to eat. After eating, we marched to another area, where we were bivouacked for a few days before receiving new orders. We set up our tents and were able to get some much-needed sleep. Before I sacked out, I checked on my squad. Most were asleep. I'm so proud of them."

"One thing I noticed was just how many soldiers were missing. Our victory was at a high cost. The ranks have indeed thinned out, but we will get replacements before the end of the week. The war was not over, but today was a great day."

JULY 27TH, 1918

"This morning, we started a few days of intense training, even though we have been fighting for the last few weeks. This training will be different. We aren't spending a lot of time training in small teams, but rather in company-sized and larger teams. I told my squad we would return to the ranges and fire our personal weapons, the machine guns, and the mortars. They all liked the idea of firing machine guns and mortars. Something different for them to do. And, of course, we can't forget about bayonet training. I'm worn out from today. There is more training tomorrow. We start at daybreak."

JULY 29TH, 1918

"Today started off very early, with a ten-mile march in full gear to the new training area. Once we arrived, we took our position near the front and had a live-fire exercise. They had targets for us to fire at. They even had a few French tanks; the bullets bounced off them with no effect. Now, when the artillery used direct fire, they were destroyed. They also showed us how to disable them by placing a hand grenade in the tracks. It might not destroy them, but they will be stopped and less lethal. As we marched back, one of the guys in the platoon started singing, "Where Do We Go from Here?" He had a great voice, and his singing made the march a little more bearable.

Once we completed the weapon training, we marched to a new area. The forest was so dense that I had to navigate using a compass. Having used a compass very few times, one of the new platoon sergeants gave everyone instructions on how to operate it. He taught us how to shoot an azimuth so we knew which direction to move. He approached me, handed me a map, and said, 'I want you to navigate your squad to this point.' I verified the point, assembled my squad, and moved out. I initially felt very confident, but the farther we moved into the forest, the denser it got. After a few hundred yards, I stopped to get my bearings. I looked behind me, and there was the platoon sergeant. I saw an expression on his face that reduced my confidence. He yelled, 'Corporal, move out. You have one minute.'

Looking at the map and my compass, we continued, but there was a blast to my right, followed by machine gun fire. We had walked into an ambush. I quickly told my squad to get on the ground. 'What are you going to do now, Corporal?' yelled the platoon sergeant. I took out my practice grenade and threw it toward the ambush, motioning for my squad to continue moving through it and returning fire.

'Stop, stop, Corporal,' the platoon sergeant yelled. The machine gun fire stopped along with the blasts. He assembled my squad in a small clearing, looked at one of my soldiers, and asked, 'The corporal here is dead. What are you going to do?'

The soldier responded, 'I, I, I, going to do what my corporal just did. I return fire and move through the kill sack.'

He walked over to me, put his hand on my shoulder, and said, 'Correct. Soldiers, your squad leader did the right thing. He didn't get bogged down and had you return fire and move through the ambush. Corporal, your land navigation is excellent. Move your squad back to the assembly area. Great job!'

It was an intense day."

July 30th, 1918

"The weather has been great up to today. It poured, but at least it was warm. All the tents were flooded, and mud was everywhere. Every piece of my equipment had mud on it. I was so frustrated that I just sat in the rain and laughed. I took off my shirt and got my soap out. One of my soldiers saw

me, approached me, and asked, 'Corporal, what are you laughing at? You haven't lost your mind, have you?'

'This is my first shower in at least a year.'

'Great idea,' he said and walked away.

We are getting ready and preparing for another operation. The replacements have arrived and will be back at full strength very soon.

Time in the rear has its advantages and disadvantages. The good thing is that we can sleep, eat well, and have time to clean equipment and train. The bad thing is that you have too much time to think. Every soldier wants to get back in the fight. We will be there very soon. Based on some of the rumors I have heard, there were numerous German patrols probing our lines, and the artillery was continuous in the distance. The French and British are taking a beating."

July 31st, 1918

"Today, we trained on how to man listening posts. My platoon sergeant told me we would be going out in front of the lines and setting up listening posts. It is very much like an observation post. I am not sure about the difference. I only know we will be in front of our lines and close to the Germans. Maybe one of the differences is that we will move the post every day. He and I already picked out five days' worth.

I'm looking forward to getting the squad back in the fight.

I started to reflect on the last few months and everything I have been through, but I often think of what you must be going through to raise our son alone. I know it can't be easy. Being a soldier's wife may be the most difficult challenge in the military. The wives are the unsung heroes of this war."

August 3rd, 1918

"The company was able to take a couple of days' leave. There is a small village close to where our tents are located. It had an excellent bakery and a couple of butchers, but there was not much meat, and I think they sold horse meat. I steered clear of that butcher. I will eat my meat at the kitchen wagons. The café my guys and I stopped at had the best coffee. Usually, I drink my

black coffee, but they have delicious creamer. We each had a pastry and sat and talked. It was an excellent opportunity to meet the new guys. They were from a replacement division and lived near each other, but didn't know each other before the Army. One was a banker, the other a policeman.

They both blended right into the squad. It's incredible how the Army can put people from different locations, religions, and backgrounds together. They're all molding into a fighting unit, each watching the other's back. I will miss that when the war ends, and I'm back home. I think it will be hard to recreate this in civilian life.

After having our coffee, we explored the village. The village hadn't been spared the war. Many of the buildings were pot-marked, or pieces of them were missing, yet they still stood—maybe as a message to the Germans: They will stand up to them no matter what they throw their way. One thing I found interesting was that there were almost no men my age around. They were either very young or were just older men. I guess the younger ones were all off fighting the Germans.

At the end of the day, I decided to be alone for a while. I found a nice park bench to sit on and reflect. As I sat there, I decided to write you a letter. I know it's been a long time since I last wrote, but I want you to understand how much I love and miss you. This time of year is the worst. I miss our time in our backyard and walking in the parks. But have no fear. We will have those days again once this is over. I don't see how the Germans can keep going based on the number of dead I have seen littering the battlefield. I'm not even sure they go and retrieve them. We try our hardest to go and get our fallen soldiers. The sorrow their German families must feel is the same as the sorrow the French, British, and our fallen soldiers feel every day. There is only one language for a broken heart."

AUGUST 5TH, 1918

"Our time in the rear is almost over. We have all our equipment ready for our next mission. The days have been beautiful after the torrential rain a couple of weeks ago. Everything has dried out but the trenches."

August 9th, 1918

"The first day in our listening post was kinda strange being out front of our lines. Before dawn, we moved through the rolls of wire in front of the trenches. It was a crescent moon, so there was not much light. It was very dark. At the same time, my squad moved out, and so did the other squads from the platoon, but they crossed into no man's land at different locations. We all had to be in pre-defined locations before sunrise to avoid being spotted. I positioned myself in the middle of the column to maintain command and control, directing the squad as we advanced through the wire. Once we crossed over it, an engineer sealed it back up. When we have to return, it wouldn't be from that spot. We moved as quickly as possible, yet we didn't want to be detected at our first location. The listening post location came into view. It was an abandoned German observation post located on top of a small hill with two trees next to it, or rather, what was left of two trees. It was a concrete square structure with a slot to fire out of and observe.

I stopped the squad and signaled one soldier to go up to the structure and ensure it was empty. The rest of the squad would cover him as he moved. He crawled up to the side facing our lines. As he arrived at the building, he stood next to the slot and listened for any movement or sounds of conversation inside. Not hearing anything, after a minute, he walked around to the front and did the same on the slot on that side of the building. As he waited, I looked down at my watch. We had five more minutes before we had to be in position. As the minutes clicked down, I heard, 'Corporal, he is signaling for us to move up.'

I glanced at him, gave him a thumbs-up, and motioned for my squad to move to the building.

We entered the building, and I couldn't believe the smell. It smelled of rotten food and human sweat. I guess the rats couldn't eat it all. Graffiti was all over the walls. One was, 'Scheiss, Krieg. Danke Kaiser Wilhelm.' I'm unsure how long this had been abandoned, but when I looked out of the slot facing our lines, I could see why the Germans selected this building. The field of view was excellent. I could see almost the entire sector with the naked eye. When I used my binoculars, I could make out some of the units in the rear.

Once we secured the area, I knew it would be a long day, so I split the squad into shifts: four men on and four off. Of the four on, two were in the building, and two were outside as sentries.

As the sun set, the battlefield took on a surreal quality. It was so quiet I could hear the screams of wounded soldiers. God knows how long they had been there, but I heard one reasonably close, so I decided to take one man with me and capture the wounded soldier. I couldn't just let him lie there and die. The other soldier and I crawled down to where the moaning was coming from; when we got there, it wasn't a German. It was one of the Moroccans who had done the reconnaissance of the area for listening posts. When we got to him, he was not wounded by a bullet or artillery but by some kind of mine that was buried in the ground. His right foot had been blown off. He was bleeding, but somehow, he had put a tourniquet on his leg to stop the bleeding, or surely he would have bled to death.

I hoisted him on my back, and we returned to the squad. As we started to move him, I heard a German patrol in the very near distance. They were moving to where the Moroccan soldier had been. I think they must have heard him, too, and under the cover of night, they were coming to capture him. But they were too late. We continued to move. I wanted as much distance as possible between them and us. I could see the building. My heart was pounding, and I gasped for air. He must have weighed over 170 pounds. The other soldier opened the back door of the building, and I ran inside. I lay him down and almost collapsed on the floor.

One of the other soldiers said, 'Damn, Corporal, we send you out for a German, and you bring home a Moroccan. Next time, bring back a girl.' I had to laugh to myself. As I lay on the floor, I heard in a whisper, 'Corporal, the Germans are right in front of us.' My mind raced over all the options. I decided on what I thought was best. We would wait to see how far the Germans would advance toward our position. If they came within striking distance, we would try to capture them. After all, we were a listening post, here to observe and remain undetected. However, if we could capture a German or two, all the better."

"Dad, you know what I noticed in his writings?"

"What's that?"

"Most of the time, he uses 'we', not 'me or I.'"

"He's a good leader and knows it's not all about him. The only way he or his men can survive is as a team."

Alex nodded and continued to read.

"The German patrol was almost upon them when they abruptly turned around and ran back toward their lines. During this entire time, one of my men treated the wounded soldier. He had his hand over his mouth so the Germans wouldn't hear screams or moans. My next dilemma was whether to take him back to the rear now or wait until our mission was over tomorrow morning. Could he survive another twelve hours?

I decided to wait. I couldn't compromise my mission for one man. I would have taken him back if they'd put me in this position a year ago, but not now. Nope, not now. If he dies, he dies.

The rest of the night was the usual, with artillery in the distance but nothing since the earlier patrol.

Just before daybreak, we left the listening post and made our way through our lines. With the Moroccan with us, he survived the night. We turned him over to the stretcher-bearers. That was a good feeling. Later in the day, the Moroccan commander sent a letter thanking us for bringing him in."

August 12th, 1918

"Well, last night was our last listening post-mission. We were scheduled to have a couple more, but new orders came down. This time, we didn't have any buildings to stay in. We were out in the open, nothing between us and the Germans but air. When we got there, I had the squad dig in and build a dirt berm in front of us.

The night started with little activity, and then around midnight, the sky was filled with light streaks as the shells went over our heads, like a sky filled with falling stars. It was a quarter moon with decent illumination. We had a great field of view, and in the distance, I could make out a platoon as they approached and moved our way. I positioned the squad along a line with the BAR in the center next to me. In our mission brief, I was ordered to fire on any element moving toward our lines. Once I commenced firing, I was to pop a red flare. So we did just that. We opened up as they moved into our kill box with the moon behind them. Within the first few seconds, we had already taken a few out. The rest fell on the ground and returned fire. As they were down, I instructed my squad to move back toward the line. As we moved, I shot off a red flare. In just a matter of minutes, our artillery started firing, sending shells in their direction. What I didn't know then but know now is that behind that initial platoon were two companies of German infantry. Our early warning allowed us to repel the planned attack.

We did such a great job. We were given a day pass to rest and relax in the village. We all got medals. I can't wait till you see me in my uniform. Then again, you might not recognize me."

AUGUST 20TH, 1918

"We just came off a divisional training mission. Every element of the division participated in this live-fire exercise. My battalion was positioned on the left flank, and my company was nearest to the enemy positions. As we dug in, the sound of artillery started, and off to my left, I heard a rumble I had never heard. Suddenly, the horse soldiers, better known as the Cavalry, rode in on their horses. My God, what a wonderful sight! The horses were so beautiful as they passed by at a full gallop. They went past my position so fast it was like lightning. The soldiers on the horses had their sabers out at the ready. They were waiting to make a deadly slash across whoever got in their way. They can attack with such speed and deadly consequences. As quickly as they rode in, they were out of sight as fast.

The rest of the exercise was standard. Once the artillery moved farther from the front lines, we got out of our concealed positions and were on the attack. When we were about halfway through No man's land came the simu-lated gas attack. We stopped in our tracks, put on our gas masks, and continued advancing. My breathing got labored while running with the mask on. It had been a while since I was in a gas attack, and I had forgotten how much I hated these masks. After we attacked the trenches, I heard the sound of 'All clear.' I removed my mask, and water poured out of it. Instead of putting it back in its pouch, I let it hang down to dry. I took out my water canteen and must have drunk half of it at one time. I looked at one of my soldiers. He was kneeling, panting like a dog. I had to start laughing. I so wanted to find a bowl and put water in it so he could drink out of it. However, my laughter was cut short when the platoon sergeant walked up and said, 'Move back to our original position. We are doing it again.'

Where we are going is going to be intense. I have never seen them train like this. I'm not laughing anymore."

CHAPTER 18

HALLOWED GROUND

ENROUTE TO THE MEUSE-ARGONNE AMERICAN CEMETERY: BELLEAU FRANCE

The drive to Meuse-Argonne American Cemetery allowed Alex to continue reading the diary. The number of pages remaining told him that he was getting to the end of his story and the unknown soldier's life.

As he started to read, he asked, "Do you think he could be buried in the cemetery?"

"Son, I'm not sure. What I do know is there are thousands of heroes buried there."

Alex turned his attention back to the diary.

AUGUST 31ST, 1918

"I had a dream, no, a nightmare last night. I relived the day Ohio was killed. We were both in the shell crater. I looked at him, and as I did, his head fell back, and blood started to pour out of the back of his head. His head bounced back. He looked at me with blood running down his face and said,

'It's true you don't hear the one that gets you. I didn't hear the one that got me. Corporal, I'm at peace. We will meet again soon.'

It was like I couldn't wake up. I tried and tried, but I couldn't escape the nightmare. When I did wake up, it was by one of my soldiers shaking me. 'Corporal, you're having a nightmare.' Sweat poured down my face when I awoke, and my hands trembled. I looked at him and replied, 'I'm all right. Bad dream. Must have been something I ate.' I could tell by the look on his face that he didn't believe one word I said. I got up and stood there for a few minutes before sitting back down. I couldn't get back to sleep, so I cleaned my rifle."

SEPTEMBER 2ND, 1918

"We arrived at our new assembly area, which, strangely enough, is one we have been to before. But this time, it was different. I could already hear the sound of artillery in the near distance. The company was all gathered as we awaited our orders. As we waited, some new soldiers filled the ranks. My squad is fully manned, so we didn't get any of them. I'm kinda glad. I don't have time to train and get them up to speed. Right now, the squad is working very well together.

My platoon sergeant approached me and said I would be promoted at the end of the month. He wanted me to take over one of the sections, and there was no way I could decline. To tell you the truth, I'm looking forward to it. He asked me who in my squad would be a good squad leader. My first thought was Ohio, but that was not to be. I told him to give me a couple of days, and I would let him know.

A sergeant? I never saw that coming—more pressure on me, but a new challenge. Well, I have to get back to the task at hand and prepare for the next battle."

SEPTEMBER 3RD, 1918

"The faces of the soldiers are ones of resolve, conviction, and determination. We all want this war to end, and the battle we are about to dive into will hopefully bring the reality of peace a little closer and this war to its

finality. I'm so proud of my soldiers, and I know they will perform in battle, like all the others, and we will have our dead comrades on our minds as we fight. We fight for them and their families. The war is not only about the Europeans. It's about much more. I can't even describe it. It's more of a feeling, and everyone feels the same way. Defeat is not an option.

Around noon today, the division commanding general came by the company, and I saw something in his eyes as he talked to the troops. We weren't just a bunch of strangers. We were his soldiers and his family, and every loss has taken a toll on him. His voice and words had power, confidence, and conviction. When he spoke, it was motivational. We all needed it. He talked to us on our level, not down to us. He may be a general, but I felt we were equal. We all die. It all depends on how and when.

After his speech, everyone had a little more pep in their steps. We were ready for the fight ahead of us. We don't know when, but you can't sustain a unit this large with just training. We sang a little louder when we marched back to our area. I feel good about myself and my soldiers. However, my nightmare the other day weighed heavily on my mind. Hence, this is the reason I want to get back in the fight. I have to make sure he was wrong.

I miss you. I can't wait for you to read my diary. I'm thinking about sending it to you, but there is so much more I will write about. Yet, when you read it, we can sit in the park, have a nice bottle of wine and some cheese, and just be together. That is my perfect day."

SEPTEMBER 5TH, 1918

"I spent the day helping the stretcher-bearer. I wanted to get some extra first aid training, so I asked my platoon sergeant, and he approved it. It also gave me a chance to break the monotony of day-to-day training and equipment cleaning.

While I was there, a young soldier was brought in. His arm was a mess. He had been hit by German machine gun fire. He must be from a different unit because I didn't think we had any units at the front just yet. I didn't want to be too close as they treated him. As I stood there, a doctor in his white coat, covered in blood, grabbed me by my sleeve and said, 'Come with me. I need you to help hold him down.' I stood there, frozen. 'Sir, I don't know what to do.'

'Corporal, hold him,' he said. 'I need to take his arm off, or he is going to die. Do you want him to die?' The look on his face said it all. He was exhausted, but there was no sleep or rest for him. More wounded soldiers arrived every minute. I ran over to the soldier and grabbed his feet. I couldn't watch it. I turned my head, but I could hear his scream as the bone saw cut through his upper arm. My god, the sound was one I had never heard, not even on the battlefield. I held his legs down with all my might. His adrenaline was pumping. It took another soldier to assist in holding his legs. I grabbed the left, and he, the right. It didn't take the doctor long. He had done this time and time again since he was in France. Nothing in his medical training could have prepared him for such a situation. It was all about saving the soldier's life. By the time he was done, they were moving the soldier to another section of the makeshift hospital or maybe another hospital in Paris.

The doctor turned to me. 'You did good, Corporal. He will live. It will be hard for him, but he will live.' He pointed to another soldier lying in the bed and said, 'He won't. There is nothing I can do, nothing.' He shook his head. I saw the pain in his eyes. He was a hero to me. I walked over to the dying soldier, knelt, grabbed his hand, and held it. I didn't say a word. What could I say? I didn't want him to be alone when he passed away. I hope I'm not. I looked up and said, 'Ohio, take care of him. He died as I held his hand.'

I got up and walked outside. I needed some fresh air. I'm not sure assisting in the hospital was a good idea, but it made me realize that no matter your job or where you are on the battlefield, everyone's job is essential. I will never forget that.

When I got back to my squad, we practiced first aid. I want to save every soldier and allow them to be cared for properly. I owe them that."

SEPTEMBER 8TH, 1918

"We only marched by night. The weather is miserable, with rain and chilly temperatures. Oh, there is mud on top of mud. We can't have any fires. We are too close to the front and don't want the German airplanes making target practice out of us. So, the only way to keep warm is to move. We are

sleeping in what we call 'Dog Tents.' They are two-man tents, a tiny A-frame tent. This all seems like déjà vu. We did the same thing a year or so ago. Not much has changed in this sector, and just as last time, we've moved so quickly that the logistics haven't kept up with us. Fresh meat is hard to find, and food, in general, is lacking."

MEUSE-ARGONNE AMERICAN CEMETERY: BELLEAU, FRANCE

"Hey, we're almost there. Leave the diary here when we walk around."

Alex nodded in agreement. As they drove on, Alex could see the visitor center to his right in Fere-en-Tardenois. Walter parked, and as they exited the car and turned toward the cemetery, they stared in amazement.

"My God, I'm at a loss for words, Dad. This place is beautiful."

Walter just nodded and wiped his eyes.

"Dad, are you okay?"

"Yes, son, there is something about soldiers. This is hallowed ground. There are 14,246 Americans buried here, both men and women, in eight different sections of the cemetery. Most of them died in the Meuse-Argonne Offensive from September through November 1918. Son, this is also the largest number of soldiers laid to rest in Europe."

Walter wrapped his arm around Alex. They walked toward the memorial chapel, situated in the center of the cemetery. As they walked, they took in the sheer number of graves, each with a white Latin cross or Star of David in perfect alignment. The grounds were immaculate, not a blade of grass out of place. Oriental plane trees and polyantha roses, along with dwarf boxwood hedges, lined the walkway. They were in no hurry. This was one place where they wanted to take their time.

"Dad, do you think he's buried here?"

"I don't know, son, but if so, I think I know where to look. In 1921, four unknown soldiers were exhumed from four different U.S. cemeteries in France. One was chosen to be placed in the Tomb of the

Unknown Soldier at Arlington. The other three unknowns are buried here."

"Could he be one of them?"

"The unknown soldier is only known to God."

"Dad, are all the American soldiers who died in World War I buried in France?"

"No, the families could have their loved one repatriated to the U.S. Between 1919 and 1922, it was done at no cost to the families. I'm not sure of the exact number, but it was a substantial amount. About 44,000."

They continued to walk toward the memorial chapel, Walter's arm around Alex. Alex did not attempt to dislodge his father's arm, and their father-son bond was growing daily. They passed the center pool and continued toward the chapel on the ridge overlooking the cemetery.

"Son, how would you like to stop by the graves of the three soldiers who weren't selected for the Tomb?" Asked Walter.

"Really, of course, Dad. Are they buried here?"

"Yes. Come on."

They walked over to Section G, in the burial plots 1, 2, and 3, where the three unknown soldiers who were not selected on Oct 23rd, 1921, lay.

Once they arrived, both just stood there with tears in their eyes. Alex put his arm around his dad and thought to himself, "He is not here."

As they were standing at the graves, the cemetery custodian walked over and said, "Excuse me, but are you Americans?"

Walter replied, "What gave it away…"

She replied, "I overheard you two talking. By the way, welcome. Is it not beautiful?"

Alex said, "Yes, we are Americans. Yes, my god, it is beautiful."

"Well, it's almost time to take the flag down. Would you like to help? Sir, I can tell you were a soldier."

"Walter is my name, and yes, I was. Alex, my son, and I would be honored to assist in lowering the Old Glory."

They all walked up the hill toward the flag close to the chapel on the hill.

At four o'clock, taps were played, and the flag was lowered. Standing at the bottom of the flagpole, waiting to catch it, was Walter. Standing at attention. As the flag was lowered to the ground, he grabbed it by the bottom corner. Alex ran over to assist, making sure the flag didn't touch the ground. Once the flag was disconnected from the halyard. Walter and Alex folded it into a triangular shape, commonly referred to as a half-cocked hat shape.

Walter handed the flag to the custodian and said, "Thank you. What a privilege."

Alex said, "Yes, thank you. Come on, Dad, let's go on in the chapel."

As they entered, they saw the flags of the principal Allied nations that fought in World War I: the United States, the United Kingdom, France, and Italy.

Alex turned his attention to the beautiful stained-glass windows. He moved closer and said, "Hey, Dad, check this window out."

"Hmm, very cool. Those are unit patches. I've seen a couple of them before. Big Red One - the First Infantry Division, Rock of the Marne - Third Infantry Division, 2nd Infantry Division, 7th Infantry Division, and a few more. I'm guessing these are all the divisions that fought in the offensive."

After spending time inside the chapel, they went outside and walked along the covered walkway. On the walls, almost a thousand names of the missing service members were inscribed. Alex and Walter each placed a hand on the wall as they passed, feeling the names as they walked.

"Dad, let's go to the visitors' center. What do you think? Do we have time?"

"Sure, we have time."

"Oh, and he's not buried here. I don't feel anything."

"Don't feel anything?" Walter quirked an eyebrow.

"Yes, sometimes I get a feeling. I can't describe it, but I felt it at the First Infantry Memorial and in a few other places we visited."

"Interesting. I'm not sure what I can do, but let's go to the visitor center."

At the visitor center, Alex opened the door. Inside were glass cabinets filled with equipment used by the soldiers. Trench knives, hand grenades, rifle magazines, and columns with individual stories from the heroes of that battle. They spent the better part of an hour going through the building. The attendant told them it was close to closing time. They thanked him and headed back to the car.

Before climbing into the car, Alex turned back toward the cemetery. "Thank you!"

Then he got in the car and waited for his dad.

CHAPTER 19

FALL OFFENSIVE

The stop at Meuse-Argonne Cemetery left a lasting impression on both of them. Its beauty and reverence were only outdone by the sheer number of graves from a single offensive. As they drove back to Paris, Alex took out the diary and started reading it again. But before he did, he asked, "Where else could he be buried? There are three other American cemeteries in France."

"Well, maybe his body was never recovered, or maybe in the States."

"Dad, are you thinking what I'm thinking?"

"Is that a trick question? What are you thinking?"

"Well, do we have extra time to fly into D.C. and visit Arlington National Cemetery before going home?"

"I would have to change our flight home, but you know what? Yes, let's do it. I'll arrange everything."

SEPTEMBER 11TH, 1918

"We moved into position tonight. It was the darkest night I have ever seen. The only sounds were those of the men moving with their equipment. Even that was quiet. Not one word was spoken. Everyone was concentrating on getting into position. As I walked among my squad, there was one common look on everyone's face. Determination.

I can't believe all the new faces in the company. We have lost so many good men, and I worry we are about to lose many more in this offensive. The soldiers who arrived in June 1917 were battle-hardened but longed to be home. I'm one of them, but not many of us are left. The attack was on the horizon—time to finish prepping and get some rest."

SEPTEMBER 12TH, 1918

"I didn't get much sleep. I'm exhausted. At 1:00 a.m. this morning, the sky turned from dark to light by our artillery shells flying overhead en route to their destination. My only hope was that they killed as many Germans as possible before we climbed out of our trenches. As the rounds impacted the German positions, the ground shook, and the rumbling from the explosions vibrated through my body. The artillery cannons fired not only high explosives but also gas. The wind was blowing out, so we didn't need to wear our masks, but we had them ready just in case.

I looked out of the trench using one of the periscopes and saw the largest explosion I have ever witnessed. One or more shells must have hit an ammunition depot. The sky lit up a bright orange, and the dirt rose in a large cloud of debris at least one hundred feet in the air, clouding and masking the horizon. It was amazing. It resembled a large tree with a long trunk and a broad, expansive canopy. As the shells impacted all along the trench line, soldiers were cheering. We were in no hurry to climb out of the trench into the wall of machine gun fire that would greet us.

Then I heard the loudest and deepest boom I had ever heard. I have no idea what guns we were using, but I can only imagine the effect the shells had on impact. The barrage lasted for hours till around sunrise. As the sun rose, the darkest night so far turned into a window of hell. The sky was ablaze with shells exploding and dirt and other debris flying through the air. The open fields were soon going to be littered with the dead, my fellow soldiers. My heart was pounding, beat after beat after beat. We were ready to come out of the shelter of our trenches and into No man's land, an all too familiar place, as we waited for the whistle to move out. I looked at my watch, and it was 5 a.m. Just then, the artillery fired smoke shells to mask our movement out of the trenches. In front of me, I could only see as far as the smoke clouds. The barren land that so many had died on previously. I hoped the Germans wouldn't see our movement, but the smoke wouldn't stop one bullet.

I heard the whistle, and on cue, we all climbed out of the trenches and ran toward the German lines. Once out of the trenches, we moved across our barbed wire. Once we were clear of it, there was nothing between us and the German defenders but air. The loud, thunderous sounds of our tanks advancing at the wire made me smile. My squad was positioned on the right flank, with two tanks flanking us on either side. We were getting closer and closer to the smoke cloud. It was a windless day, so the smoke just hung there. The artillery continued to pound the German lines while we moved. With each step, I looked over at my squad, counted each one, and, at the same time, prayed for each of them. Thank God everyone was holding in formation as we advanced.

We reached our first objective mostly unscathed. Our casualties were on their way to the dressing stations.

Our next objective was the unmanned German trenches. But there was one main obstacle—a fast-flowing river. When we came upon the river, our artillery stopped to allow the engineers to put their footbridges in the water so we could cross. The engineers did a flawless job preparing and putting the bridges in the water. No time was lost. My squad crossed the river, where the river was shallow, and the tanks crossed. On the other side, we regrouped and continued moving to the next objective.

Once we reached our second objective, we encountered minimal resistance. My squad was intact so far. However, when we advanced to the third objective, the familiar sound of German artillery could be heard.

Boom, boom, boom, German shells fell from the sky behind me. They had yet to get their range right because of the thick cloud of smoke in front of them. Their forward observers were blind. Overhead, I could hear the sound of airplanes. I didn't know if they were ours or the Germans'. They sounded like they were circling overhead in front of us. No sooner than the shells started impacting, machine guns opened up. The Germans had the perfect placement for their machine guns. I looked to my left, and soldiers started to fall one after another, sometimes two at once. The wall of bullets was almost impenetrable. The yellow field of hay gave way to a thick forest. I knew in my head that there was no way the tanks would make it through. It would be hard enough for a foot soldier. The Germans had ample time to set out booby traps. By this time, one of my soldiers lay dead in the field. I didn't have time to go to him. We had to make it to the woods if we wanted to survive.

My squad skirted the wood line and started firing on the machine gun emplacements. Another squad came up behind us and fired as we moved. We then moved as they fired. We continued until the other squad was close enough to take them out with hand and rifle grenades. The Germans who weren't killed were taken prisoner. They were brought to the dressing stations if they needed treatment. If anything, we are a nation of caring people, even for the enemy.

We didn't have time to bask in our glory. We got orders to continue to the next objective. So far, I was only down one man.

I assembled my squad and prepared to move when the platoon sergeant approached me and said, 'I need you to take the remaining men of this squad along with yours.' I now had almost a squad and a half. The other squad had taken a beating.

As we got closer to the objective, another river became an obstacle. It was so steep along the banks that some of the tanks got bogged down and could not cross. The remaining tanks had to find another fording point.

Word came down that the Germans were about to launch a counterattack. My squad was ordered to move to the left flank. When we got into position, I felt the ground under my feet begin to rumble, not the same as from the tanks; this was more of a fast-moving wave. I looked to my left, and the most magnificent sight I had ever seen came into view. Beautiful, majestic horses running into battle, with their cavalry soldiers on top of them in a full gallop, with their swords out, yelling 'Charge.' The speed of their attack caught the Germans off guard.

I could hear machine gun fire to my left. I hurried my squad to the next terrain feature where we could fire on the Germans and assist the mounted cavalry. We had to cross over the German wire, but we made it. I was not ready for what lay before my eyes. Horses on the ground, their lives cut short by German machine gun fire. I couldn't hold my emotions. I have seen way too much death, but the sight of those beautiful animals will forever be in my mind. I wept. I couldn't control my emotions, not for the soldiers. They knew what they signed up for, but for the horses. Have I lost empathy for man?"

September 13th, 1918

"Today was another tough day. The company was repositioned, which required us to march through some very dense forest. I'm glad I picked up the compass and land navigation quickly. My squad was put in at the lead. Not only was the forest dense, but it was also dark and gloomy. In addition to the thick forest and the darkness, the Germans placed many obstacles in our way. Some we could remove, and some we marked and went around. The lesson I learned in those days stuck with me. I didn't want to get sucked into an ambush. We spent hours moving through the forests. It seemed there was one after another. Now, these forests are different. There are many trees, but the years of war have reduced many of them to stumps. There are not many branches or leaves; the artillery just destroys the tops of the trees. I wonder if they will ever grow normally again. Will lush forests replace the crater-ridden, leafless trees in the future? Can the land become healthy again after all the mutations and gas laid upon it? Something I wonder about myself. Will I ever be normal again?

As we came out of the forest onto what was once a very nice road, the German snipers started firing at us. One of my soldiers was wounded but not killed. He was hit in the right shoulder. He was lucky. If it had been his left, he would more than likely be dead. We treated them as best we could, and the stretcher-bearer moved up and took him back to the treatment tent. I will have to check on him once we reach our objective, or should I say, I will try.

Before we knew it, we were way ahead of the rest of the units. We made our way through marshes, forests, open fields, pockmarked with shell craters, and in and over trenches. Now we wait on the rest of the unit before the Germans figure out we are all alone."

SEPTEMBER 14TH, 1918

"Thank God we, the rest of the unit, moved up to our position, and once there, the entire unit was relieved by another, so we could go back and regroup and prep for the next battle. I couldn't believe what I saw as we moved back through the forest. The Germans had built a very nice rest camp. There were showers, kitchens, and enclosed sleeping areas. Home away from home. Now, the German officers had moving picture machines, pianos, and other luxuries. They had even built cottages for the officers. Of course, every one of the rooms and cottages was furnished when they looted the nearby towns. The Germans left in such haste that kitchens and uniforms were left behind. I don't think they ever thought they would have to abandon the forest. But they had no idea who they were up against. We kicked their butts out of the forest, and now we are enjoying their luxuries. I don't think we would stand for the difference between how the German army treats the officers and enlisted men—they're treated like second-class citizens.

Well, one thing is consistent. No matter where we rest, there are always delousing stations. I hate the lice more than the Germans. You return to the trenches as soon as you get rid of them, and they are all over you. I don't even scratch anymore. What good does it do? The horses were quartered near the delousing stations, but there were not as many as before. I still can't get the picture out of my mind of seeing those horses slaughtered. I went over and petted a couple of them. It was the most soothing experience I have had since I got here. We might get a couple when I get home.

I went to the medical tent to find my soldier, but they said he had already been moved to a hospital. He had an infection and a bad cold or influenza. I turned to exit and noticed there were a lot of soldiers in beds. None of them looked wounded. I asked one of the stretcher-bearers why the soldiers were in bed. He replied, 'They have been coming into the treatment center in waves, all with the same symptoms: high fever, dry cough, headaches, body aches, chills, running nose.' I told him it sounded like a cold. He replied, 'Corporal, this ain't no cold. Soldiers die daily. Today and yesterday, more soldiers have died from this influenza than from combat injuries.' He turned his back, put his hand into a sack, and pulled out a handful of cloth masks. 'Do you have any of these?'

'No.'

'Here, give these to your men and have them wear them when close to others, no matter who. Is this enough, or do you need more?'

I counted them and said, 'This is plenty.'

'Corporal, I suggest you put one on now.' As I started to walk out of the room, I noticed a white sheet on the ceiling. I asked him what it was for. He said, 'To show moving pictures, it helps them relax.'"

"Dad, did you hear what I just read? Is he talking about COVID-19?"

"Without knowing it, he's talking about the outbreak of the Spanish Flu."

"Okay, I remember hearing about it during Covid time, but it wasn't from Spain, was it?"

"No, the first recorded outbreak was, I believe, in Kansas at Camp Funston, which is now Fort Riley. From there, it spread with the troops across the Atlantic. The flu killed thousands of soldiers fighting in Europe on all sides of the war, not just the Americans. It devastated units that were needed to fight. They had to consolidate units to have enough soldiers to complete the mission."

"Wow, he has seen it all. But yet he, along with all the other soldiers, fought on. By the way, how many service members died from the Spanish flu in World War I?"

"Damn, you're really trying to test my knowledge. If I remember correctly, it was around 45,000. Hell, son, there were over 53,000 deaths from combat. Just think about that—it's crazy."

"So, not only did they have to worry about getting shot or blown up, but they also had to worry when someone sneezed on them. What made it so different from the normal flu?"

"Good question. The average age of a soldier in World War I was twenty-six. That's young. The Spanish Flu was most deadly in young people, not the elderly or very young, unlike the normal flu. Typically, it wasn't the flu but secondary infections, normally in the lungs. But you're right. They had the Germans and the flu to worry about."

"I returned to my squad, handed out the masks, and told them they needed to wear them in small, confined areas. They all looked at me like I was crazy. Then, one of my soldiers started to cough. I ordered him to the treatment tent. Everyone put their mask on. They didn't need another reminder. It's time to rest and clean the equipment again. The war waits for no one. Well, since we are in a great place to relax and prep for the next orders, the weather is now the enemy. Even though it's mid-September, it's cold and rainy. It's not a downpour, but rather a constant drizzle. Everything is damp, but free of lice and rat remnants.

I decided to visit one of the German cottages. It had a piano, and a German prisoner was playing it. Everyone was very cheerful, even the German prisoner. His war was over; ours, well, no one knows. If I were a prisoner of the Germans at the end of the war, I would rather fight on and die in combat. I see how they treat their own so differently from regular soldiers in their army. I'm sure it wouldn't be pleasant."

SEPTEMBER 15TH, 1918

"I went to church services today. I need to reconnect with God. This war has made me a hollow man. I need him back in my life. Before I went, I asked if any of my squad wanted to join me, but only one new soldier accepted. He had just gotten to the unit and was assigned to my squad two days ago. We haven't had an opportunity to talk. As we walked, I asked him how long he had been in the Army. He replied, 'I was drafted a few months ago, caught the flu when I arrived in France, and was bedridden for a couple of weeks.' He was from Texas and worked on a family ranch outside Fort Worth. His brother joined the Army in 1917, before the draft, and was killed at Soissons.

I remembered Soissons. It seemed like a long time ago, but it was only a few months ago. So many good men were lost, and one of them was his brother. I didn't know him based on his last name, but I could hear the pain in his voice. We continued with small talk until we arrived at the area where the service would be held. It was one of only a handful of beautiful places in the forest. Some of the trees had leaves, and they were beginning to change color. What was once a dark green leaf was now a vibrant mix of orange, red, and yellow. I just stood there for a bit and looked at them. One leaf started to fall to the ground. I watched it the entire way as it floated effortlessly to the ground. With a gentle nudge of the wind, it would turn in a circle as it descended. I was at peace and more relaxed than I had been in months. There is so much I want to do when I get home. Some people may find the things I want to do trivial, but to me, they represent the essence of life. My soldier continued walking till he realized I had stopped. He stepped back, tapped me on the shoulder, and asked, 'Corporal, what are you doing?' I replied, 'Living.'

We found a place to sit, and more soldiers were attending the service than I would have thought. The chaplain was already standing there at his improvised pew. The theme of the service was giving thanks for our victories. We remembered the ones we lost and those who were wounded and prayed for their speedy recovery. He talked about praying over a dying German soldier who was next to a dead American soldier he had killed. He said he had rage like any normal human being, but he was compelled to pray for the German soldier. There was no more harm he could inflict. He knew nothing about him other than that he was a child of God. We sang a few hymns and prayed a lot. I prayed for you and our son. That's all I can do from here. Pray and pray. The chaplain closed the service, and we walked back to our area. I had a good feeling the rest of the day. I picked up a leaf."

SEPTEMBER 16TH, 1918

"Today, the mail came, and many letters went out. Thank you for not writing. My squad took an excursion to an area that gave us a view of the battlefield. It looks a little different from above. The panoramic view was amazing. It was so tranquil, but the sound of artillery could be heard in the distance, bringing me back to reality. It won't be long before we are the target of the artillery. A couple more of my men came down with influenza, so I'm a couple short for now. There are not many replacements since most of them are sick. What's worse? A prolonged death from influenza, dying from German mustard gas, getting blown up, or being shot? I guess the best is to avoid all of them."

SEPTEMBER 20TH, 1918

"We all boarded French troop trains. Remember the Cattle Car? Well, we had another ride on one of those. This time, it wasn't too bad. The ride was during the night, and we arrived at dawn. When we got out of the train car, the dawn was spectacular. The sun was beginning to rise, with thin, high clouds and a mild breeze. It would have been very easy to fall in love with this place if it didn't smell of death. We have a lot of prep to do before we go back into battle. Everyone is upbeat and ready to show the Germans again what we are made of. Between here and where we were, I lost my identification disks. I will have to get some new ones as soon as possible. If anything happens to me, I don't want to be placed in an unknown grave.

My squad is escorting the company commander to our location on the battlefield, where we will be taking over. We are going to recon the route we will be taking, including all the bridges. Will be doing that for the next few days."

September 25th, 1918

"I don't know how many miles we walked, but it was a lot. I'm glad we got a ride back on one of the supply trucks going to the rear from the front line. Even though we didn't have to walk. The ride in the back of one of those trucks was no fun.

As we walked along the route, I saw signs of previous battles everywhere I looked. Crosses beside the dirt roads indicated where a soldier or soldiers were buried. There were even sticks with hats and helmets on them. Along the road, discarded equipment and bandages were everywhere. There were still smoldering stumps in some places. I could feel the pain and suffering with every step. As we made our way into what was left of a once beautiful French village, my commander came up to me and said, 'Do you want to hear a great story?' Well, not for missing out on a good story. I replied, 'Yes, sir.'

'A couple of months ago, this village was controlled by the Germans. There must have been hundreds of them. A French armored car, I think it was a Peugeot, was on the German side of the village with its crew. As the situation for the crew drew dire, the sergeant in charge decided they would drive through the middle of the town, firing their pistols as they raced through the streets. To get back to their lines. The Germans were so surprised

that they didn't even fire back. They couldn't believe what they were seeing. An enemy armored car drove through the city and also shot at them as they drove. After making it to their lines, the commander asked how they got there, and they told their story. They all were awarded Croix de Guerre and given a couple of days in the rear.'

Once he was done, I looked at him and said, 'Sir, please, are you pulling my leg?'

'No, Corporal, they drove on this street we are standing on.'

After we made our way through the village, we came upon a river. In the distance, I could see a half-completed bridge. I'm guessing that was one that the Germans started to build. I'm pretty sure we will try to finish it. As I approached the river, the current was fairly swift, and debris was scattered everywhere, including wooden poles, boxes, wagons, animals, and even human remains. The water was a greenish black color, not a natural color for such a beautiful place. Even though there were bridges we could use to cross, we looked for fording locations. We found a couple of places at each bridge we could ford. It would take additional time, but they would allow us to cross and get into our positions. We marked all the bridges on my map and identified those that needed repair. This list was turned in to the engineering company to determine if they could be repaired.

During one of the breaks, the captain approached me and said, 'I forgot to mention. I heard you were getting promoted.' I replied, 'Yes, sir, that is what I have been told.'

'You're going to make a good sergeant.'

'I'm not too sure about being a good sergeant. I don't know if I want to take on additional responsibility. I can't turn the promotion down, can I?'

He turned and laughed."

September 26th, 1918

"Well, the battle is getting closer. I can hear the artillery fire. What a wonderful sound since we were in the trenches. They are prepping the battle-field, and it won't be long until we can hear them and see the impact of the shells. Tonight, we are going back into the forest and practicing navigating by compass and some other assault drills."

CHAPTER 20

BODIES IN THE BARBED WIRE

Back at their hotel in Paris, they only had one day to visit Versailles and the Compiègne Wagon. Alex could see by the thickness of the remaining pages that the unknown soldier's story was almost finished. He never jumped ahead in the diary, and his last entry would surprise both of them.

"So, tomorrow we're going to Versailles and the Compiègne Wagon. How does that sound?"

"Dad, that sounds like a great way to end our adventure. Now, I did a little investigation into the Compiègne Wagon. Did you know that not only was the armistice for World War I signed in it, but also the armistice signed on June 22nd, 1940? That one ended the fighting between the Germans and the Third French government in France. The French resistance fought on. They didn't adhere to the armistice."

"Now that is interesting."

"That's not the half of it. After the Nazis took control of France, Hitler had it moved to Berlin, where it was displayed in a large city park. When the Allies drew near to Berlin, it was relocated to a small town in Thuringia, between Coburg and Erfurt, Germany, for safekeeping. However, the SS, not wanting it to be used for another humiliating surrender by the Germans, destroyed it. What we are going to see tomorrow is a copy."

"Wow, Alex. I'm impressed."

"Thank you." He sauntered over for a hug.

"Dad, we have a few minutes before dinner. Can I read a little more?"

"Absolutely."

September 30th, 1918

"Well, all the training is finished for this upcoming battle. All our equipment was inspected, and any items that were not 100% were replaced. The nights are getting colder. It will be winter very soon. My feet are already cold.

A couple more soldiers fell ill with influenza today. We are down five guys in my squad, and the rest of the company is not much better. They are going to have to consolidate some units together until we get our soldiers back —well, the ones who don't die. I can't imagine what is happening to the Germans. I hope they can't muster enough men to fight back.

When I look into the eyes of my fellow soldiers, the brightness is gone, and the spark is missing. We have seen enough death and destruction in a year and a half for a lifetime. But we will fight on with our last breath."

October 1st, 1918

"Instead of living in the trenches, we are all in our two-man foxholes. They don't provide much cover, but it's better than lying in the open. I'm just glad the ground is not frozen. There would have been no way we could have dug the foxholes. Some of the soldiers just dug in the shell craters, making them deeper. I didn't want to do that. They were filled with water, rats, and who knows what else.

Last night, I was assigned to another company. We lost too many men to influenza. I hope they don't know I'm scheduled to get promoted. Maybe this is a good thing. I would rather stay with the men from my squad.

I heard the artillery setting up behind me. By the sound of the movement, there are hundreds of cannons. It's going to get loud. I'm sure by the time they start to fire, I will be on the frontlines. Once everyone was in place, I checked in on them. They know what lies ahead, yet they're ready for the fight. I told them that at least one person must always be awake in the foxhole and take two-hour shifts. Tomorrow will be the start of many long days of fighting."

OCTOBER 3RD, 1918

"Last night, I went on a recon patrol looking for weak points in the German lines. It felt good getting out of the foxhole. There were four of us in my patrol. We exited our lines with the help of the engineers. They cleared a path through all the barbed wire and other obstacles. Once we cleared our lines, they were sealed again. I looked at my watch. We had to be back at the location we had crossed in four hours. We might not have been able to get back through the defenses if we had been late. We encountered some of their obstacles as we got closer to the Germans. They were formidable, but we found a weak point. I marked it on my map and moved on. We went through the weak point and came upon a German observation post. As we got closer, we could hear them talking. One of the soldiers with me spoke German. I brought him up and asked him to translate. He said he needed to get closer to determine what they were saying precisely. I looked at him and asked if he was nuts. They are fifteen feet away now. He shrugged. Not the response I thought I would get. I almost laughed out loud.

We took off all our equipment and left our rifles. We took only our trench knives. We needed to be within ten feet of them, and by God, we were going to get that close. He and I moved into position on the downward slope of the OP so we couldn't be detected. We lay there and listened to them. After a few minutes, he tapped me on the shoulder and whispered, 'They are pretty mad. They were discussing how sick everyone was getting, and they had to stay at the OP for longer than planned. One said he was a cook. Why was he on the front lines? Other than that, they didn't say much.'

I said, 'Let's go.' We returned to the rest of the patrol, and to my right, flares lit up the sky. The next thing was the sound of machine gun fire. We froze in our tracks. So far, we hadn't been detected, but that didn't last long. Bullets started flying all around us, not like they knew we were there. It was random firing, hoping to hit us. It must have been the cook. I ordered the patrol to continue to move back to our lines. We only had thirty minutes left to get through. In front of me, one of the soldiers stopped.

I crawled up to him. The machine gun fire had hit him. He was bleeding from at least three strikes, with one to his chest. I could hear the gurgling sound of air leaving his lungs, but I was not going to leave him. I gave my rifle to another soldier, grabbed him by his equipment, and pulled him as I crawled. Then I felt a hand touch the hand that I was holding onto him with. I stopped. He was trying to say something. I put my ear close to his mouth, 'Leave me, Corporal, please.' Those were his last words, but I couldn't let him go. As we got closer to our lines, another soldier ran back to me as the machine gun rounds started impacting again. He took hold of the dead soldier and carried him back. I got up and ran after him, bullets impacting all around. Once we were all back on our side and under cover, I went over to the dead soldier, took his identification disk, and put one in my pocket.

I found my platoon sergeant, gave him the disk, and told him everything we heard the Germans say. I also gave him the map with the weak point of the German defenses. He patted me on the back and told me to get some rest. The look in his eyes told me more than to get some rest. I learned later that the patrols that went out had significant casualties and were beyond our wire in No man's land. Commanders were trying to figure out how to rescue them if it was possible at all.

As I was walking back to my squad's position, I could see that the tanks were ready to move. Very impressive, but loud."

OCTOBER 4TH, 1918

"The morning started with an artillery barrage right in front of our positions. It's almost too close. I could feel the blast as I lay in my foxhole. I heard the whistle to prepare to advance. I poked my head out of the foxhole to ensure my squad was ready to move. A minute later, the whistle sounded, signaling it was time to move out. We all got out of our foxholes and started to move. As soon as we did, the German machine guns sent a wall of bullets toward us.

Soldiers fell left and right of me, but I kept moving, and my squad was with me. The artillery shifted its fire closer to the Germans, but that didn't stop the wall of bullets. Dirt was flying all around me from the rounds impacting. It took a few minutes to make it to the barbed wire. It was a shocking sight. Dead American soldiers lay tangled in the wire. They were the bodies of last night's patrols. Their lifeless bodies told the story of their last moments of life. Riddled with bullets, the anguish in their faces made me feel dizzy. All this death is having an effect on me. As we crossed the wire, one of my soldiers was hit and fell into the wire next to another soldier.

I could see the German trenches in front of me. I started to run faster. I jumped over the trench berm, and as I was in the air, I moved my rifle around and had the bayonet facing down. I landed on top of a German soldier, piercing him in the chest with my bayonet. As it entered his chest, I heard his last breath. I took the bayonet out and stabbed him again. As I stabbed him again, I looked up, and a German soldier was pointing his rifle at me. I was ready to die. I wanted my war to end. He never fired the weapon. One of my soldiers was behind him and plunged his trench knife into his back, and his rifle hit the ground. I heard the soldier say, 'Corporal, are you all right?'

I nodded and continued to move in the trench. As I passed him, I patted him on his back and said, 'Thank you.' We linked up with the rest of the squad. All were in heated hand-to-hand combat, well, all but one. I assigned him a Winchester Model 1897 shotgun. He leveled the shotgun and fired two shells, taking out three Germans. He continued to move down the trench, firing and killing as he moved. The remaining Germans fled the trench and were met with hand grenades. We fought for hours before reaching our objective. Luckily, I only lost one in my squad. I use the word lucky. What has happened to me? One of my soldiers is dead, and I'm the lucky one?

As we mopped up the area, the CO gave me a new mission for tomorrow. I'm going to be part of a group of soldiers from different platoons to verify a route along our right flank. I need to link up with them before tomorrow. I love you."

Alex looked up. "Dad, that was his last entry." A tear formed in his eye. He closed the diary, walked over to his father, and gave him a hug.

"Are you okay?"

"I'm not sure. I knew he was going to die, but I didn't want his story to end. In the back of my mind, I wanted him to live. I wanted a happy ending, just like in the movies. I want him to live, go home, have kids, grow old, and die in the arms of a loved one. Not like he died. Alone on the battlefield in a country thousands of miles away from home."

"He didn't die alone. He died with his fellow soldiers. They all meet at Fiddler's Green."

Hugging his dad tight, Alex said, "Let's just hang around Paris tomorrow. Then get ready for our flight home."

CHAPTER 21

THE CHANGING OF THE SENTINEL

ARLINGTON NATIONAL CEMETERY: ARLINGTON, VIRGINIA

After deciding to visit Arlington National Cemetery, Walter and Alex stepped off their flight from Paris. After reading the soldier's diary, they chose to pay their respects to America's fallen. They left the airport and jumped on a bus to their car rental. Once they got in the car and drove to Arlington National Cemetery, they took Highway 267 and merged onto 66. After a few miles, they went on the George Washington Memorial Parkway along the Potomac River. Then, they turned off the parkway into the entrance to Arlington National Cemetery.

There was a trolley they could have taken that would have taken them through the cemetery, but they decided to walk and pass through fields of America's heroes on foot. It was an easy one-mile walk to the Tomb of the Unknown Soldier. They started with the Bible and the unknown soldier's diary in hand. In addition to the Bible and diary, they stopped to buy extra-large Ziplock bags, a notepad, and envelopes before arriving at the cemetery.

Alex turned to his dad. "I didn't know this was so big."

His father nodded. "I don't know much about it, but I believe it's over 600 acres, and over 400,000 are buried here."

They walked down Roosevelt Drive. Alex could see the Memorial Amphitheater on the horizon. They took a right on Wilson Road, walked by the Space Shuttle Columbia Memorial, a little past the Memorial Amphitheater, and stopped at Audie Murphy's gravesite.

Alex noticed a red rose on Audie Murphy's headstone. "Dad, why is there a red rose on his headstone?"

"Good question. Every time I have come here, there's always a fresh rose. I need to ask someone."

After a few minutes, they walked over to the viewing area for the changing of the sentinel. As it was early October, the changing of the sentinel occurred every hour on the hour.

Walter looked at his watch. "Fifteen minutes before the change." They were both excited. Walter had seen the changing of the guard at least twice before, but this one was special. Not only because his son was with him, but also because it was his son's first. They were bringing a piece of history with them, maybe the soldier's diary buried in the tomb.

TOMB OF THE UNKNOWN SOLDIER, ARLINGTON NATIONAL CEMETERY: ARLINGTON

As they approached the viewing steps, Alex said, "I can't believe everything is in line, no matter how you look." Alex could feel the presence of the unknown soldier, but he didn't say anything to his dad.

Once they reached the viewing area, they saw a crowd of spectators forming, waiting to see the sentinels change. It was a perfect day, with mild temperatures, light wind, and blue skies. They decided to stand along the railing next to the Imperial Danby marble wall.

Reading the diary over the last few days was life-changing for both of them. They relived the life of someone they had never met and didn't know, but somehow, they felt a connection. Maybe it was because Walter was in the Army and could relate to the life of a soldier in combat. It was almost therapeutic for him—a history lesson from the words of someone who lived it.

For Alex, it was like watching a movie through the words of a soldier. Sometimes, after reading a section, he could close his eyes and see the entire scene play out in his head. There were times he would have to open his eyes to stop the sheer brutality of war. But yet, he knew he had to finish the diary. He had to learn what the soldier's last written words were. It's like time was frozen when he put the last period in the final sentence the soldier wrote.

At precisely the top of the hour, the relief commander arrived, dressed in an impeccable uniform. She appeared in the plaza and announced the change of the sentinels. The new sentinel walked out of the tomb guard quarters and unlocked the bolt of his M14 rifle—a signal to the relief commander to begin the ceremony. The relief commander walked to the tomb, turned toward it, and saluted. She then turned to the spectators and said, "Please stand for the ceremony and remain standing and silent."

Alex got goosebumps, and a sense of pride overwhelmed him. His dad looked over and smiled. He, too, had goosebumps.

On the far end of the plaza, the new sentinel stood at attention while the relief commander walked over to him and started a detailed white-glove inspection of his uniform, equipment, and weapon, up one side of him and down the other. A more thorough inspection couldn't be found in the Army.

The inspection of the weapon was meticulous. Every part was inspected for cleanliness and proper working order. Once the inspection was completed, the relieving sentinel and the relief commander met the retiring sentinel at the center of the black mat in front of the tomb. All three turned and saluted the unknown soldier, who had all been symbolically given the Medal of Honor. After they finished the salutes, the relief commander ordered the relieved sentinel, "Post and orders, remain as directed."

The newly posted sentinel replied, "Orders acknowledged," and stepped into position on the black mat.

The relief commander passed the new sentinel and began walking at a pace of ninety steps per minute. The tomb sentinel marched exactly twenty-one steps down the black mat behind the tomb as the relieved sentinel and the relief commander turned to the tomb guard quarters.

Once the ceremony was over and the crowd thinned out, they sat on the steps, and Alex pulled out the Bible and diary from his backpack. He opened the diary, did a double-take at the last entry, and looked at his father in a trembling voice. "Dad, look at the date. It's today, October 4th. His last entry was 105 years ago today."

Walter scanned the entry and couldn't believe it. They hadn't connected the dates. As they sat there, they knew they had renewed their love for one another, and a father-and-son bond was forged in steel, never to be broken.

"Well, I guess it's time, Dad."

"Yep, I think it is."

Alex took a notepad and a pen out of his backpack and started writing.

"Whoever finds this Bible, look inside. There, you will find the first-hand account of an unknown U.S. soldier who fought in World War I. The diary was hidden in the Bible in a secondhand bookstore in Paris until this year. The Bible was found hidden behind a stack of books. Who put it there? We don't know, nor did the young lady at the bookstore. What is known are the words in this diary that moved my dad and me to retrace some of the soldier's journey as he fought in the war. It tells the story of a brave man who loved his country, his fellow soldiers, and the men he led. Nowhere does it mention his name, unit, place of origin, or any other personal information.

Inside the diary is a note we found when we opened it. It tells the day, year, and circumstances of the soldier's death and how the diary was recovered.

We don't know who wrote the letter, but as you read it, whoever found it wanted everyone to know the soldier may be unknown, but is not forgotten."

Alex put the note in front of the Bible and then put the diary back. Then he put the Bible in the Ziploc bag. They stood, turned around, walked toward the tomb guard quarters, placed it by the door, and walked off. After over a hundred years, the soldier who died on the field of battle in 1918 and his diary were finally reunited.

As they lay it down, the faint sound of taps could be heard in the distance. Another hero was being laid to rest. They put their hands over their hearts and waited until the taps ended. Walter turned to his son and said, "I love you, Alex, and always have. I know it's been tough."

"I love you, too, Dad. I never stopped loving you. I'm sorry for causing pain. That won't happen again."

Walter grabbed his son, held him tight against his chest, and said, "Son, I missed you."

Alex looked up and smiled, a tear running down his cheek, not saying a word. Everything he needed to say was in his eyes.

As they walked off, a sense of calm came over them. In a tree, they heard the sound of a morning dove. They looked up, and the bird seemed to nod its head.

Walter put his arm around Alex and smiled.

Alex said, "Come on, Dad. Let's go home. Mom is waiting for both of us."

THE END

POSTSCRIPT

There was no way for Sergeant Younger to know whose remains were in each one of the caskets. However, the casket he selected carried the remains of a soldier he saw in a war-torn field in France on an early fall day in October 1918.

Walter and Alex purchased a diary in a secondhand bookstore in Paris. The diary was written by a young soldier buried in the Tomb of the Unknown Soldier. The words written in the diary pages would forever change their lives. So moving were the words that they set them on a path to visit the Tomb of the Unknown Soldier and leave the Bible and diary next to the Memorial Amphitheater.

The bond that grew out of a son and father reading the day-to-day struggles of a soldier would never be broken and would only grow stronger over time. They would pay their respects at Arlington National Cemetery and the Tomb of the Unknown Soldier every year. It was the same type of bond that the young soldier felt for his fellow soldiers as he wrote his diary.

It was a bitterly cold winter day in 1918. A twenty-year-old woman sat crying at her kitchen table with a telegram in her trembling hands. The tears hadn't stopped since she got the telegram. Even in small towns, news of the war traveled fast. Yesterday, she received word from the War Office that her husband was missing in combat in France. What was she to do? He was her life. They grew up together and married young. He joined the Army to support his family before the war began. She wanted him home. What was she to do? She missed him so.

She got up from the table, walked over to her writing desk, opened the drawer, and pulled out a letter dated August 3rd, 1918. It was his last letter to her, and she started to cry again.

On a cold November day in 1921, the same woman took her young son to Washington, D.C., to pay their respects to the hero's casket that lay in state in the Capitol Rotunda. As they passed the casket, a sense of calm overtook her, and a chill went up her back. The last time she felt that calm was the day before her husband left for the Army many years ago. She could hear his voice in her head, "I'm okay, I don't hurt, and I'm at peace. Live your life. I will always love you and our son." Her knees buckled, and her five-year-old son looked at her and asked, "Mommy, are you all right?"

She replied, smiling, "Yes, son. I'm good; no, I'm great. Let me tell you about your father."

Until then, she had only mentioned his father on rare occasions. She thought it would be too hard on him. In the years that followed, she would remarry. She found a man who loved her son as much as she did. She died in 1950, still yearning for her missing husband, but she knew he was among America's heroes from that day, November 10th, 1921, when she and her son paid their respects to the unknown soldier.

On a cloudy fall day in October 1918, in a field, a young French girl's actions and compassion for the soldiers who traveled thousands of miles and fought to save her country started a chain of events that changed so many lives, including hers, a father, a son, a future director of the Central Intelligence Agency, and a future president. Witnessing and participating in heroic actions in combat led to the awarding of the Medal of Honor to a young lieutenant. That young, carefree soldier and his written words were finally home after a journey of over one hundred years and thousands of miles to a place called The Tomb of the Unknown Soldier at Arlington National Cemetery.

In 1932, the completed Tomb of the Unknown Soldier was unveiled. The marble sarcophagus was placed above the grave of the unknown soldier from World War I. The sarcophagus was engraved with elaborate carvings of wreaths on the north and south sides. On the east side of the sarcophagus, three neoclassical figures representing peace, victory, and virtue are depicted. On the west of the sarcophagus is the inscription:

"HERE RESTS IN
HONORED GLORY
AN AMERICAN
SOLDIER
KNOWN BUT TO GOD."

GLOSSARY

Aluminum Identification Disks – Small aluminum disks with the soldier's name, regiment, and religion. Today, they are commonly referred to as "dog tags." Each soldier carried two. One would remain with the deceased soldier, and the other was taken as proof of death.

Artillery battery – Four cannons under the command of a captain. The battery was divided into two cannons led by a lieutenant.

Azimuth – Refers to compass points from 0 ° to 360 °. 90° is east, 180° is south, 270° west and 360° is north. Soldiers used a map and an azimuth to navigate from one point to another.

Bangalore Torpedoes – An explosive charge used to clear obstacles. The explosive charge can be a single tube or multiple tubes connected.

Blitzkrieg – *"Lightning War,"* a military strategy used by Germany in the early days of WWII. The strategy combined armor, infantry, artillery, and air assets to overwhelm enemy armies in short, decisive campaigns.

Browning Automatic Rifle (BAR) – A family of American-made semi-automatic and automatic rifles. The rate of fire for the BAR was 500 – 650 rounds per minute. It was first introduced in WWI in the late summer of 1918. One BAR was assigned per squad.

Bunker-buster, the 37mm M1916 – Used by U.S. soldiers to destroy German machine gun nests. It was equipped with a telescopic sight for better accuracy.

Bayonet – A sharp-edged knife designed to fit on the end of a rifle.

Commanding Officer (CO) – The leader of a company/battery/troop-sized unit. Normally, a captain. However, in aviation units, the CO might be a major.

Entrenching Tool (E-Tool) – A small shovel used by soldiers to dig foxholes and carried on their backpacks.

Fiddler's Green – A term used by modern-day cavalry units to memorialize the deceased. Fiddler's Green was a fire support base in the Vietnam region III, 1972, manned by the 2nd Squadron, 11th Armored Cavalry.

French Chasseurs – A term for hunters, it was applied to light infantry French and Belgian units, as well as light cavalry units. Troops trained to be able to engage the enemy rapidly.

French Resistance – A collection or groups that fought the Nazi occupation of France in World War II.

First Sergeant (E8) – The highest-ranking enlisted soldier in a company, troop, or battery in the U.S. Army. The first sergeant reports to the commanding officer and is responsible for maintaining discipline and overseeing the day-to-day operations of the unit.

Forward Observer (FO) – A soldier or soldiers who provide advanced warning of enemy troop activity and movement, then report it back to their unit.

Gewehr 98 – Rifle used by German troops in World War I.

Grid Coordinates – Used to find a particular point or location on a map. The location can be within 1000 meters or as precise as 10 meters.

German SS – Schutzstaffel, a paramilitary wing and elite guard organized under Hitler and the Nazi Party.

German U-boats – Is a slang name for German submarines.

Gestapo – The office secret state police of the Nazi party within Germany and its occupied countries.

Kitchen Police (KP) – Additional duties other than cooking are given to soldiers to assist in the mess hall or dining facilities.

Line of Departure (LD) – An imaginary line used for an attacking army to start the attack. Units are required to cross the LD at specific times.

Livres – French for a book. Soldiers in WWI kept personal books as a means to release frustration, fears, and their experiences.

M1 gas mask – A piece of equipment issued to U.S. soldiers to protect them against chemical attacks (gas).

M1917 Browning machine gun– A heavy machine gun used by the U.S. forces in WWI, WWII, Korea, and Vietnam. The M1917 fired a 7.62 NATO round.

M1911 .45 cal Pistol – Standard issue sidearm for the U.S. Military from 1911 – 1985.

MG08/15 – Maschinegewehr 08, the standard German machine gun used in WWI.

Mausers – A bolt-action rifle designed by Peter Paul Mauser initially in 1871.

Mustard Gas – A human-made sulfur mustard that causes blistering skin and mucous membranes on contact. Large doses were fatal in WWI. It can also cause chronic respiratory disease and permanent blindness.

Noncommissioned Officer (NCO) – The backbone of any unit, responsible for maintaining morale and training of the individual and small unit training. NCO rank is E5–E9. In certain situations, an E4 can be given the rank of corporal and is considered an NCO.

No man's land – An area between opposing armies. A term commonly used in World War I.

Observation Post – An area close to the enemy lines that soldiers use to observe and report on enemy activity and movement.

P-38 – A World War II, single-seat, twin piston-engine fighter built by Lockheed.

Platoon Leader – Normally, a 2nd lieutenant leads a platoon and is the officer's first leadership position.

Prone position – A firing position where a soldier lies flat on the ground. The most accurate position to fire from.

Salient – An elongated protrusion of a territory surrounded on three sides.

Stahlhelm helmet - The German combat helmet was first introduced in World War I. In service till 1992.

Stokes mortar – A smooth-bore metal tube with a metal base plate. Invented by Sir Wilford Stokes and used by the British, U.S., and Portuguese in the latter half of World War I.

Trench Knife—A combat knife used to kill or wound in close combat. It was perfect for trench warfare in World War I. The M1917 was the American version of the knife and featured a knuckle guard.

Yperite – Mustard gas or Sulphur mustard

1917 Enfields – Formally named "United States Rifle." It's a .30 caliber rifle used in World War I.

1903 Springfields – A five-round feed, bolt-action, .30 caliber rifle. It was the standard issue before the introduction of the 1917 Enfield.

BIBLIOGRAPHY

- The First World War – A Complete History – Martin Gilbert
- History of the First Infantry Division – The John C Winston Company – 1922
- United States Army in the War 1917 – 1919 – Military Operations and of the American Expeditionary Forces – Volume Four
- Tomb of the Unknown Soldier Had Its Origins in World War I – US Department of Defense
- Society of the Honor Guard – https://tombguard.org/
- KU Medical Center – Medicine in the First World War – Gas in the Great War
- First Infantry Division Museum – https://www.fdmuseum.org/
- History of Fort Riley and the First Infantry Division
- Arlington National Cemetery – The Changing of the Guard – arlingtoncemetery.mil
- American War Memorials Overseas – uswarmemorials.org
- American Battle Monuments Commission – Meuse Argonne American Cemetery
- Numerous Wikipedia articles
- The Art of World War 1 – By Ephraim Durnst
- World War 1 – The Definitive Visual History – Smithsonian
- Uniforms & Equipment of the Central Powers in World War 1 – Dr. Spencer Anthony Coil

ABOUT THE AUTHOR

Travis Davis is an Air Force brat who grew up in Arkansas, Spain, New York, and California. He joined the U.S. Army at 17 years old as an Armored Reconnaissance Specialist and was stationed at various forts in the United States and Germany, where he met his beautiful wife. During his three tours in Germany, he conducted hundreds of border patrols along the East-West German border and the Czechoslovakia-West German border. He saw firsthand communism and its oppression of its citizens. He retired from the U.S. Army, where his last duty assignment was as Assistant Operations Sergeant of the 2nd Armored Cavalry Regiment at Fort Polk, Louisiana. He is a lifetime member of the Sergeant Morales Club. Travis has also received multiple awards, including the Meritorious Service Medal and five Army Commendation Medals.

When he is not writing or working, Travis enjoys exercising, traveling (he loves a good road trip), baking different loaves of bread, making ice cream, and relaxing in his backyard with friends and family while having a cold beer. He lives in Allen, Texas, with his wife, Martina. They have been married for 39 years. He has three adult children: two daughters living in Arkansas and one son living in Northern Virginia, as well as eight wonderful grandchildren.

"Travis never met a stranger," his wife always says.

ALSO BY TRAVIS DAVIS

Flames of Deception

An imagery analyst at the National Geospatial Agency (NGA) analyzing imagery of the oil fields in Western Siberia identifies strange behavior in the oil fields. His keen eye uncovers the best-kept secret in modern history. His intelligence sparked a chain reaction, leading the U.S. government to launch a multi-agency clandestine operation into the matter. At the same time, Russia, China, and India were preparing to conduct the largest naval and ground assault in modern history (codename Bia) to control the transportation of oil through strategic choke points and stop the free flow of oil on land and at sea worldwide. With the help of North Korea, China is planning the most expansive cyber attack on the United States' "Green Energy" power grid. The potential for World War III is real. Can it be stopped?

War on the Porch: A Doughboy's Interview

In 1968, a local reporter was writing a story for one of Arkansas's newspapers about the upcoming 50th anniversary of the end of **World War I**. The reporter, Gordon Grover, set out to interview local veterans, including Patrick King, a veteran who had been blinded during the war by an artillery attack. Initially, Patrick hesitated to speak with the reporter and participate in the interview until he learned that Gordon was a **World War II** veteran and that his father had fought and died in World War I. With his wife, Pauline, by his side, Patrick shares his story, which turns into a journey of healing. In 1968, a local reporter was writing a story for one of Arkansas's newspapers about the upcoming 50th anniversary of the end of **World War I**. The reporter, Gordon Grover, set out to interview local veterans, including Patrick King, a veteran who had been blinded during the war by an artillery attack. Initially, Patrick hesitated to speak with the reporter and participate in the interview until he learned that Gordon was a World War II veteran and that his father had fought and died in World War I. With his wife, Pauline, by his side, Patrick shares his story, which becomes a journey of healing. The narrative he shares describes how a patrol of ordinary soldiers, against all odds, achieved the extraordinary by carrying out a nearly impossible mission behind German lines in northern France in July 1918, just as the Second

Battle of the Marne was about to begin. It is an incredible tale of heroism, bravery, leadership, selflessness, and perseverance that has never been told because General Pershing advised Patrick in the summer of 1918 not to share it with anyone, as no one would believe him. He stayed committed to keeping it to himself until that fateful summer of 1968.